PENGUIN BOOKS

THE ABBESS OF CREWE

Muriel Spark was born and educated in Edinburgh, and spent some years in Central Africa. She returned to Britain during the war and worked in the Political Intelligence Department of the Foreign Office. She subsequently edited two poetry magazines, and her published works include critical biographies of nineteenth-century figures, and editions of nineteenth-century letters. Her *Collected Poems 1* and *Collected Stories 1* were published in 1967. Since she won an *Observer* short-story competition in 1951 her creative writings have achieved international recognition (they are published in twenty different languages). Among many other awards she has received the Italia Prize and the James Tait Black Memorial Prize. She was awarded the O.B.E. in 1967.

Mrs Spark became a Roman Catholic in 1954. She has one son.

Her first novel, *The Comforters*, was published in 1957 and this was followed by *Robinson* (1958), *The Go-Away Bird and Other Stories* (1958), *Memento Mori* (1959), *The Ballad of Peckham Rye* (1960), *The Bachelors* (1960), *Voices at Play* (1961), *The Prime of Miss Jean Brodie* (1961), adaptations of which have enjoyed long and successful runs on the West End stage and the screen, *The Girls of Slender Means* (1963), *The Mandelbaum Gate* (1965), *The Public Image* (1968), *The Driver's Seat* (1970), *Not to Disturb* (1971), *The Hothouse by the East River* (1973), *The Abbess of Crewe* (1974), *The Takeover* (1976) and *Territorial Rights* (1979).

Her play, *Doctors of Philosophy*, was first produced in London in 1962 and published in 1963.

MURIEL SPARK

The Abbess of Crewe

PENGUIN BOOKS

PENGUIN BOOKS

Published by the Penguin Group
Penguin Books Ltd, 27 Wrights Lane, London W8 5TZ, England
Viking Penguin, a division of Penguin Books USA Inc.
375 Hudson Street, New York, New York 10014, USA
Penguin Books Australia Ltd, Ringwood, Victoria, Australia
Penguin Books Canada Ltd, 2801 John Street, Markham, Ontario, Canada L3R 1B4
Penguin Books (NZ) Ltd, 182–190 Wairau Road, Auckland 10, New Zealand

Penguin Books Ltd, Registered Offices: Harmondsworth, Middlesex, England

First published in the United States of America by The Viking Press 1974
First published in Great Britain by Macmillan Ltd 1974
Published in Penguin Books 1975
7 9 10 8

Copyright © Copyright Administration Limited, 1974

Printed in England by Clays Ltd, St Ives plc
Set in Monotype Baskerville

Acknowledgment is made to the following for permission to quote material:
The Literary Trustees of Walter de la Mare and The Society of Authors as their
representative for material from 'Miss/T.' by Walter de la Mare.
Macmillan Publishing Co., Inc., A. P. Watt & Son, M. B. Yeats,
Anne Yeats, and the Estate of W. B. Yeats for material from 'Nineteen Hundred
and Nineteen,' copyright 1928 by Macmillan Publishing Co., Inc.,
copyright © Georgie Yeats, 1956; for 'He Remembers Forgotten Beauty',
copyright 1906 by Macmillan Publishing Co., Inc., copyright 1934 by
William Butler Yeats. Both poems from *Collected Poems*
by William Butler Yeats.
New Directions Publishing Corp. and Messrs Faber & Faber for
'In Durance' from *Personae* by Ezra Pound, copyright 1926 by Ezra Pound.
Random House, Inc., and Messrs Faber & Faber for material from
'Lay your sleeping head, my love' from *Collected Shorter Poems 1927–1957*
by W. H. Auden, copyright 1940 by W. H. Auden,
copyright © W. H. Auden, 1968.

Come let us mock at the great
That had such burdens on the mind
And toiled so hard and late
To leave some monument behind,
Nor thought of the levelling wind . . .

Mock mockers after that
That would not lift a hand maybe
To help good, wise or great
To bar that foul storm out, for we
Traffic in mockery.

From W. B. Yeats,
'Nineteen Hundred and Nineteen'

Chapter 1

'WHAT is wrong, Sister Winifrede,' says the Abbess, clear and loud to the receptive air, 'with the traditional keyhole method?'

Sister Winifrede says, in her whine of bewilderment, that voice of the very stupid, the mind where no dawn breaks, 'But, Lady Abbess, we discussed right from the start — '

'Silence!' says the Abbess. 'We observe silence, now, and meditate.' She looks at the tall poplars of the avenue where they walk, as if the trees are listening. The poplars cast their shadows in the autumn afternoon's end, and the shadows lie in regular still file across the pathway like a congregation of prostrate nuns of the Old Order. The Abbess of Crewe, soaring in her slender height, a very Lombardy poplar herself, moving by Sister Winifrede's side, turns her pale eyes to the gravel walk where their four black shoes tread, tread and tread, two at a time, till they come to the end of this corridor of meditation lined by the secret police of poplars.

Out in the clear, on the open lawn, two men in dark police uniform pass them, with two Alsatian dogs pulling at their short leads. The men look straight ahead as the nuns go by with equal disregard.

After a while, out there on the open lawn, the Abbess speaks again. Her face is a white-skinned English skull,

7

beautiful in the frame of her white nun's coif. She is forty-two in her own age with fourteen generations of pale and ruling ancestors of England, and ten before them of France, carved also into the bones of her wonderful head. 'Sister Winifrede,' she now says, 'whatever is spoken in the avenue of meditation goes on the record. You've been told several times. Won't you ever learn?'

Sister Winifrede stops walking and tries to think. She strokes her black habit and clutches the rosary beads that hang from her girdle. Strangely, she is as tall as the Abbess, but never will she be a steeple or a tower, but a British matron in spite of her coif and her vows, and that great carnal chastity which fills her passing days. She stops walking, there on the lawn; Winifrede, land of the midnight sun, looks at the Abbess, and presently that little sun, the disc of light and its aurora, appears in her brain like a miracle. 'You mean, Lady Abbess,' she says, 'that you've even bugged the poplars?'

'The trees of course are bugged,' says the Abbess. 'How else can we operate now that the scandal rages outside the walls? And now that you know this you do not know it so to speak. We have our security to consider, and I'm the only arbiter of what it consists of, witness the Rule of St Benedict. I'm your conscience and your authority. You perform my will and finish.'

'But we're something rather more than merely Benedictines, though, aren't we?' says Sister Winifrede in dark naïvety. 'The Jesuits – '

'Sister Winifrede,' says the Abbess in her tone of lofty calm, 'there's a scandal going on, and you're in it

8

up to the neck whether you like it or not. The Ancient Rule obtains when I say it does. The Jesuits are for Jesuitry when I say it is so.'

A bell rings from the chapel ahead. It is six o'clock of the sweet autumnal evening. 'In we go to Vespers whether you like it or whether you don't.'

'But I love the Office of Vespers. I love all the Hours of the Divine Office,' Winifrede says in her blurting voice, indignant as any common Christian's, a singsong lament of total misunderstanding.

The ladies walk, stately and tall, but the Abbess like a tower of ivory, Winifrede like a handsome hostess or businessman's wife and a fair week-end tennis player, given the chance.

'The chapel has not been bugged,' remarks the Lady Abbess as they walk. 'And the confessionals, never. Strange as it may seem, I thought well to omit any arrangement for the confessionals, at least, so far.'

The Lady Abbess is robed in white, Winifrede in black. The other black-habited sisters file into the chapel behind them, and the Office of Vespers begins.

The Abbess stands in her high place in the choir, white among the black. Twice a day she changes her habit. What a piece of work is her convent, how distant its newness from all the orthodoxies of the past, how far removed in its antiquities from those of the present! 'It's the only way,' she once said, this Alexandra, the noble Lady Abbess, 'to find an answer always ready to hand for any adverse criticism whatsoever.'

As for the Jesuits, there is no Order of women Jesuits. There is nothing at all on paper to reveal the mighty pact between the Abbey of Crewe and the Jesuit hierarchy, the overriding and most profitable pact. What Jesuits know of it but the few?

As for the Benedictines, so closely does the Abbess follow and insist upon the ancient and rigid Rule that the Benedictines proper have watched with amazement, too ladylike, both monks and nuns, to protest how the Lady Abbess ignores the latest reforms, rules her house as if the Vatican Council had never been; and yet have marvelled that such a great and so Benedictine a lady should have brought her strictly enclosed establishment to the point of an international newspaper scandal. How did it start off without so much as a hint of that old cause, sexual impropriety, but merely from the little misplacement, or at most the theft, of Sister Felicity's silver thimble? How will it all end?

'In these days,' the Abbess had said to her closest nuns, 'we must form new monastic combines. The ages of the Father and of the Son are past. We have entered the age of the Holy Ghost. The wind bloweth where it listeth and it listeth most certainly on the Abbey of Crewe. I am a Benedictine with the Benedictines, a Jesuit with the Jesuits. I was elected Abbess and I stay the Abbess and I move as the Spirit moves me.'

Stretching out like the sea, the voices chant the Gregorian rhythm of the Vespers. Behind the Abbess, the stained-glass window darkens with a shadow, and the outline of a man climbing up to the window from the outside forms against the blue and the yellow of the glass. What does it matter, another reporter trying to find his way into the convent or another photographer as it might be? By now the scandal occupies the whole of the outside world, and the people of the press, after all, have to make a living. Anyway, he will not get into the chapel. The nuns continue their solemn chant while a faint grumble of voices outside the window faintly penetrates the chapel for a few moments. The police dogs start to bark, one picking up from the other in a loud litany of their own. Presently their noises stop and evidently the guards have appeared to investigate the intruder. The shadow behind the window disappears hastily.

These nuns sing loudly their versicles and responses, their antiphons:

Tremble, O earth, at the presence of the Lord;
at the presence of the God of Jacob
Who turned the rock into pools of water:
and the strong hills into fountains of water.
  Not to us, O Lord, not to us, but to thy name, give
glory: because of thy mercy and thy faithfulness.

But the Abbess is known to prefer the Latin. It is said that she sometimes sings the Latin version at the same time as the congregation chants the new reformed English. Her high place is too far from the choir for the nuns to hear her voice except when she sings a solo part. This evening at Vespers her lips move with the others but discernibly at variance. The Lady Abbess, it is assumed, prays her canticles in Latin tonight.

She sits apart, facing the nuns, white before the altar. Stretching before her footstool are the green marble slabs, the grey slabs of the sisters buried there.

Hildegarde lies there; Ignatia lies there; who will be next?

The Abbess moves her lips in song. In reality she is chanting English, not Latin; she is singing her own canticle, not the vespers for Sunday. She looks at the file of tombs and, thinking of who knows which occupant, past or to come, she softly chants:

> *Thy beauty shall no more be found,*
> *Nor, in thy marble vault, shall sound*
> *My echoing song; then worms shall try*
> *That long-preserved virginity . . .*

The cloud of nuns lift their white faces to record before the angels the final antiphon:

> *But our God is in heaven:*
> *he has done all that he wished.*

'Amen,' responds the Abbess, clear as light.

Outside in the grounds the dogs prowl and the guards patrol silently. The Abbess leads the way from the chapel to the house in the blue dusk. The nuns, high nuns, low nuns, choir nuns, novices and nobodies, fifty in all, follow two by two in hierarchical order, the Prioress and the Novice Mistress at the heels of the Abbess and at the end of the faceless line the meek novices.

'Walburga,' says the Abbess, half-turning towards the Prioress who walks behind her right arm; 'Mildred,' she says, turning to the Novice Mistress on her left, 'go and rest now because I have to see you both together between the Offices of Matins and Lauds.'

Matins is sung at midnight. The Office of Lauds, which few convents now continue to celebrate at three in the morning, is none the less observed at the Abbey of Crewe at that old traditional time. Between Matins and Lauds falls the favourite time for the Abbess to confer with her nearest nuns. Walburga and Mildred murmur their assent to the late-night appointment, bowing low to the lofty Abbess, tall spire that she is.

The congregation is at supper. Again the dogs are howling outside. The seven o'clock news is on throughout the kingdom and if only the ordinary nuns had a wireless or a television set they would be hearing the latest developments in the Crewe Abbey scandal. As it is, these nuns who have never left the Abbey of Crewe since the day they entered it are silent with their fish pie at the refectory table while a senior nun stands at the corner lectern reading aloud to them. Her voice is nasal, with a haughty twang of the hunting country stock from which she and her high-coloured complexion have at one time disengaged themselves. She stands stockily, remote from the words as she half-intones them. She is reading from the great and ancient Rule of St Benedict, enumerating the instruments of good works:

To fear the day of judgement.
To be in dread of hell.
To yearn for eternal life with all the longing of our soul
To keep the possibility of death every day before our eyes.
To keep a continual watch on what we are doing with our life.
In every place to know for certain that God is looking at us.

When evil thoughts come into our head, to dash them at once on Christ, and open them up to our spiritual father.

To keep our mouth from bad and low talk.

Not to be fond of talking.

Not to say what is idle or causes laughter.

Not to be fond of frequent or boisterous laughter.

To listen willingly to holy reading.

The forks make tiny clinks on the plates moving bits of fish pie into the mouths of the community at the table. The reader toils on . . .

Not to gratify the desires of the flesh.

To hate our own will.

To obey the commands of the Abbess in everything, even though she herself should unfortunately act otherwise, remembering the Lord's command: 'Practise and observe what they tell you, but not what they do.' – Gospel of St Matthew, 23.

At the table the low nuns, high nuns and novices alike raise water to their lips and so does the reader. She replaces her glass . . .

Where there has been a quarrel, to make peace before sunset.

Quietly, the reader closes the book on the lectern and opens another that is set by its side. She continues her incantations:

A frequency is the number of times a periodic phenomenon repeats itself in unit time.

For electromagnetic waves the frequency is expressed in cycles per second or, for the higher frequencies, in kilocycles per second or megacycles per second.

A frequency deviation is the difference between the maximum instantaneous frequency and the constant carrier frequency of a frequency-modulated radio transmission.

Systems of recording sound come in the form of variations of magnetization along a continuous tape of, or coated with, or impregnated with, ferro-magnetic material.

In recording, the tape is drawn at constant speed through the airgap of an electromagnet energized by the audio-frequency current derived from a microphone.

Here endeth the reading. Deo gratias.

'Amen,' responds the refectory of nuns.

'Sisters, be sober, be vigilant, for the Devil goes about as a raging lion, seeking whom he may devour.'

'Amen.'

The Abbess of Crewe's parlour glows with bright ornaments and brightest of all is a two-foot statue of the Infant of Prague. The Infant is adorned with its traditional robes, the episcopal crown and vestments embedded with such large and so many rich and gleaming jewels it would seem they could not possibly be real. However, they are real.

The Sisters, Mildred the Novice Mistress and Walburga the Prioress, sit with the Abbess. It is one o'clock in the morning. Lauds will be sung at three, when the congregation arises from sleep, as in the very old days, to observe the three-hourly ritual.

'Of course it's out of date,' the Abbess had said to her two senior nuns when she began to reform the Abbey with the winsome approval of the late Abbess Hildegarde. 'It is absurd in modern times that the nuns should have to get up twice in the middle of the night to sing the Matins and the Lauds. But modern times come into a historical context, and as far as I'm concerned history doesn't work. Here, in the Abbey of Crewe, we have discarded history. We have entered the sphere, dear Sisters, of mythology. My nuns love it. Who doesn't yearn to be part of a myth at whatever the price in comfort? The monastic system is in revolt throughout the rest of the world, thanks to historical development. Here, within the ambience of mythology, we have consummate satisfaction, we have peace.'

More than two years have passed since this state of peace was proclaimed. The Abbess sits in her silk-covered chair, now, between Matins and Lauds, having freshly changed her white robes. Before her sit the two black senior sisters while she speaks of what she has just seen on the television, tonight's news, and of that Sister Felicity we have all heard about, who has lately fled the Abbey of Crewe to join her Jesuit lover and to tell her familiar story to the entranced world.

'Felicity,' says the Abbess to her two faithful nuns, 'has now publicly announced her conviction that we have eavesdropping devices planted throughout our property. She's demanding a commission of inquiry by Scotland Yard.'

'She was on the television again tonight?' says Mildred.

'Yes, with her insufferable charisma. She said she

forgives us all, every one, but still she considers as a matter of principle that there should be a police inquiry.'

'But she has no proof,' says Walburga the Prioress.

'Someone leaked the story to the evening papers,' says the Abbess, 'and they immediately got Felicity on the television.'

'Who could have leaked it?' says Walburga, her hands folded on her lap, immovable.

'Her lax and leaky Jesuit, I dare say,' the Abbess says, the skin of her face gleaming like a pearl, and her fresh, white robes falling about her to the floor. 'That Thomas,' says the Abbess, 'who tumbles Felicity.'

'Well, someone leaked it to Thomas,' says Mildred, 'and that could only be one of the three of us here, or Sister Winifrede. I suggest it must be Winifrede, the benighted clot, who's been talking.'

'Undoubtedly,' says Walburga, 'but why?'

' "Why?" is a fastidious question at any time,' says the Abbess. 'When applied to any action of Winifrede's the word "why" is the inscrutable ingredient of a brown stew. I have plans for Winifrede.'

'She was certainly instructed in the doctrine and official version that our electronic arrangements are merely laboratorial equipment for the training of our novices and nuns to meet the challenge of modern times,' Sister Mildred says.

'The late Abbess Hildegarde, may she rest in peace,' says Walburga, 'was out of her mind to admit Winifrede as a postulant, far less admit her to the veil.'

But the living Abbess of Crewe is saying, 'Be that as

it may, Winifrede is in it up to the neck, and the scandal stops at Winifrede.'

'Amen,' say the two black nuns. The Abbess reaches out to the Infant of Prague and touches with the tip of her finger a ruby embedded in its vestments. After a space she speaks: 'The motorway from London to Crewe is jammed with reporters, according to the news. The A51 is a solid mass of vehicles. In the midst of the strikes and the oil crises.'

'I hope the police are in force at the gates,' Mildred says.

'The police are in force,' the Abbess says. 'I was firm with the Home Office.'

'There are long articles in this week's *Time* and *Newsweek*,' Walburga says. 'They give four pages apiece to Britain's national scandal of the nuns. They print Felicity's picture.'

'What are they saying?' says the Abbess.

'*Time* compares our public to Nero who fiddled while Rome burned. *Newsweek* recalls that it was a similar attitude of British frivolity and neglect of her national interests that led to the American Declaration of Independence. They make much of the affair of Sister Felicity's thimble at the time of your election, Lady Abbess.'

'I would have been elected Abbess in any case,' says the Abbess. 'Felicity had no chance.'

'The Americans have quite gathered that point,' Walburga says. 'They appear to be amused and rather shocked, of course, by the all-pervading bitchiness in this country.'

'I dare say,' says the Abbess. 'This is a sad hour for

England in these, the days of her decline. All this public uproar over a silver thimble, mounting as it has over the months. Such a scandal could never arise in the United States of America. They have a sense of proportion and they understand Human Nature over there; it's the secret of their success. A realistic race, even if they do eat asparagus the wrong way. However, I have a letter from Rome, dear Sister Walburga, dear Sister Mildred. It's from the Congregation of Religious. We have to take it seriously.'

'We do,' says Walburga.

'We have to do something about it,' says the Abbess, 'because the Cardinal himself has written, not the Cardinal's secretary. They're putting out feelers. There are questions, and they are leading questions.'

'Are they worried about the press and publicity?' says Walburga, her fingers moving in her lap.

'Yes, they want an explanation. But I,' says the Abbess of Crewe, 'am not worried about the publicity. It has come to the point where the more we get the better.'

Mildred's mind seems to have wandered. She says with a sudden breakage in her calm, 'Oh, we could be excommunicated! I know we'll be excommunicated!'

The Abbess continues evenly, 'The more scandal there is from this point on the better. We are truly moving in a mythological context. We are the actors; the press and the public are the chorus. Every columnist has his own version of the same old story, as it were Aeschylus, Sophocles or Euripides, only of course, let me tell you, of a far inferior dramatic style. I read

19

classics for a year at Lady Margaret Hall before switching to Eng. Lit. However that may be – Walburga, Mildred, my Sisters – the facts of the matter are with us no longer, but we have returned to God who gave them. We can't be excommunicated without the facts. As for the legal aspect, no judge in the kingdom would admit the case, let Felicity tell it like it was as she may. You cannot bring a charge against Agamemnon or subpoena Clytemnestra, can you?'

Walburga stares at the Abbess, as if at a new person. 'You can,' she says, 'if you are an actor in the drama yourself.' She shivers. 'I feel a cold draught,' she says. 'Is there a window open?'

'No,' says the Abbess.

'How shall you reply to Rome?' Mildred says, her voice soft with fear.

'On the question of the news reports I shall suggest we are the victims of popular demonology,' says the Abbess. 'Which we are. But they raise a second question on which I'm uncertain.'

'Sister Felicity and her Jesuit!' says Walburga.

'No, of course not. Why should they trouble themselves about a salacious nun and a Jesuit? I must say a Jesuit, or any priest for that matter, would be the last man I would myself elect to be laid by. A man who undresses, maybe; but one who unfrocks, no.'

'That type of priest usually prefers young students,' Walburga observes. 'I don't know what Thomas sees in Felicity.'

'Thomas wears civilian clothes, so he wouldn't unfrock for Felicity,' observes Mildred.

'What I have to decide,' says the Abbess, 'is how to

answer the second question in the letter from Rome. It is put very cautiously. They seem quite suspicious. They want to know how we reconcile our adherence to the strict enclosed Rule with the course in electronics which we have introduced into our daily curriculum in place of book-binding and hand-weaving. They want to know why we cannot relax the ancient Rule in conformity with the new reforms current in the other convents, since we have adopted such a very modern course of instruction as electronics. Or, conversely, they want to know why we teach electronics when we have been so adamant in adhering to the old observances. They seem to be suggesting, if you read between the lines, that the convent is bugged. They use the word "scandals" a great deal.'

'It's a snare,' says Walburga. 'That letter is a snare. They want you to fall into a snare. May we see the letter Lady Abbess?'

'No,' says the Abbess. 'So that, when questioned, you will not make any blunder and will be able to testify that you haven't seen it. I'll show you my answer, so that you can say you have seen it. The more truths and confusions the better.'

'Are we to be questioned?' says Mildred, folding her arms at her throat, across the white coif.

'Who knows?' says the Abbess. 'In the meantime, Sisters, do you have any suggestions to offer as to how I can convincingly reconcile our activities in my reply?'

The nuns sit in silence for a moment. Walburga looks at Mildred, but Mildred is staring at the carpet.

'What is wrong with the carpet, Mildred?' says the Abbess.

Mildred looks up. 'Nothing, Lady Abbess,' she says.

'It's a beautiful carpet, Lady Abbess,' says Walburga, looking down at the rich green expanse beneath her feet.

The Abbess puts her white head to the side to admire her carpet, too. She intones with an evident secret happiness:

> *No white nor red was ever seen*
> *So amorous as this lovely green.*

Walburga shivers a little. Mildred watches the Abbess's lips as if waiting for another little quotation.

'How shall I reply to Rome?' says the Abbess.

'I would like to sleep on it,' says Walburga.

'I, too,' says Mildred.

The Abbess looks at the carpet:

> *Annihilating all that's made*
> *To a green thought in a green shade.*

'I,' says the Abbess, then, 'would prefer not to sleep on it. Where is Sister Gertrude at this hour?'

'In the Congo,' Walburga says.

'Then get her on the green line.'

'We have no green line to the Congo,' Walburga says. 'She travels day and night by rail and river. She should have arrived at a capital some hours ago. It's difficult to keep track of her whereabouts.'

'If she has arrived at a capital we should hear from her tonight,' the Abbess says. 'That was the ar-

22

rangement. The sooner we perfect the green line system the better. We should have in our laboratory a green line to everywhere; it would be convenient to consult Gertrude. I don't know why she goes rushing around, spending her time on ecumenical ephemera. It has all been done before. The Arians, the Albigensians, the Jansenists of Port Royal, the English recusants, the Covenanters. So many schisms, annihilations and reconciliations. Finally the lion lies down with the lamb and Gertrude sees that they remain lying down. Meantime Sister Gertrude, believe me, is a philosopher at heart. There is a touch of Hegel, her compatriot, there. Philosophers, when they cease philosophizing and take up action, are dangerous.'

'Then why ask her advice?' says Walburga.

'Because we are in danger. Dangerous people understand well how to avoid it.'

'She's in a very wild area just now, reconciling the witch doctors' rituals with a specially adapted rite of the Mass,' Mildred says, 'and moving the old missionaries out of that zone into another zone where they are sure to be opposed, probably massacred. However, this will be an appropriate reason for reinstating the orthodox Mass in the first zone, thus modifying the witch doctors' bone-throwing practices. At least, that's how I see it.'

'I can't keep up with Gertrude,' says the Abbess. 'How she is so popular I really don't know. But even by her build one can foresee her stone statue in every village square: Blessed Mother Gertrude.'

'Gertrude should have been a man,' says Walburga. 'With her moustache, you can see that.'

'Bursting with male hormones,' the Abbess says as she rises from her silk seat the better to adjust the gleaming robes of the Infant of Prague. 'And now,' says the Abbess, 'we wait here for Gertrude to call us. Why can't she be where we can call her?'

The telephone in the adjoining room rings so suddenly that surely, if it is Gertrude, she must have sensed her sisters' want from the other field of the earth. Mildred treads softly over the green carpet to the adjoining room and answers the phone. It is Gertrude.

'Amazing,' says Walburga. 'Dear Gertrude has an uncanny knowledge of what is needed where and when.'

The Abbess moves in her fresh white robes to the next room, followed by Walburga. Electronics controlroom as it is, here, too, everything gleams. The Abbess sits at a long steel desk and takes the telephone.

'Gertrude,' says the Abbess, 'the Abbess of Crewe has been discussing you with her Sisters Walburga and Mildred. We don't know what to make of you. How should we think?'

'I'm not a philosopher,' says Gertrude's deep voice, philosophically.

'Dear Gertrude, are you well?'

'Yes,' says Gertrude.

'You sound like bronchitis,' says the Abbess.

'Well, I'm not bronchitis.'

'Gertrude,' says the Abbess, 'Sister Gertrude has charmed all the kingdom with her dangerous exploits, while the Abbess of Crewe continues to perform her part in the drama of *The Abbess of Crewe*. The world

24

is having fun and waiting for the catharsis. Is this my destiny?'

'It's your calling,' says Gertrude, philosophically.

'Gertrude, my excellent nun, my learned Hun, we have a problem and we don't know what to do with it.'

'A problem you solve,' says Gertrude.

'Gertrude,' wheedles the Abbess, 'we're in trouble with Rome. The Congregation of Religious has started to probe. They have written delicately to inquire how we reconcile our adherence to the Ancient Rule, which as you know they find suspect, with the laboratory and the courses we are giving the nuns in modern electronics, which, as you know, they find suspect.'

'That isn't a problem,' says Gertrude. 'It's a paradox.'

'Have you time for a very short seminar, Gertrude, on how one treats of a paradox?'

'A paradox you live with,' says Gertrude, and hangs up.

The Abbess leads the way from this room of many shining square boxes, many lights and levers, many activating knobs, press-buttons and slide-buttons and devices fearfully and wonderfully beyond the reach of a humane vocabulary. She leads the way back to the Infant of Prague, decked as it is with the glistening fruits of the nuns' dowries. The Abbess sits at her little desk with the Sisters Walburga and Mildred silently composed beside her. She takes the grand writing-paper of the Abbey of Crewe and places it before her. She takes her pen from its gleaming holder and writes:

'Your Very Reverend Eminence,

Your Eminence does me the honour to address me, and I humbly thank Your Eminence.

I have the honour to reply to Your Eminence, to submit that his sources of information are poisoned, his wells are impure. From there arise the rumours concerning my House, and I beg to write no more on that subject.

Your Eminence does me the honour to inquire of our activities, how we confront what Your Eminence does us the honour to call the problem of reconciling our activities in the field of technological surveillance with the principles of the traditional life and devotions to which we adhere.

I have the honour to reply to Your Eminence. I will humbly divide Your Eminence's question into two parts. That we practise the activities described by Your Eminence I agree; that they present a problem I deny, and I will take the liberty to explain my distinction, and I hold:

That Religion is founded on principles of Paradox.

That Paradox is to be accepted and presents no Problem.

That electronic surveillance (even if a convent were one day to practise it) does not differ from any other type of watchfulness, the which is a necessity of a Religious Community; we are told in the Scriptures "to watch and to pray", which is itself a paradox since the two activities cannot effectively be practised together except in the paradoxical sense.'

'You may see what I have written so far,' says the

Abbess to her nuns. 'How does it strike you? Will it succeed in getting them muddled up for a while?'

The black bodies lean over her, the white coifs meet above the pages of the letter.

'I see a difficulty,' says Walburga. 'They could object that telephone-tapping and bugging are not simply an extension of listening to hearsay and inviting confidences, the steaming open of letters and the regulation search of the novices' closets. They might well say that we have entered a state where a difference of degree implies a difference in kind.'

'I thought of that,' says the Abbess. 'But the fact that we have thought of it rather tends to exclude than presume that they in Rome will think of it. Their minds are set to liquidate the convent, not to maintain a courtly correspondence with us.' The Abbess lifts her pen and continues:

'Finally, Your Eminence, I take upon myself the honour to indicate to Your Eminence the fine flower and consummation of our holy and paradoxical establishment, our beloved and renowned Sister Gertrude whom we have sent out from our midst to labour for the ecumenical Faith. By river, by helicopter, by jet and by camel, Sister Gertrude covers the crust of the earth, followed as she is by photographers and reporters. Paradoxically it was our enclosed community who sent her out.'

'Gertrude,' says Mildred, 'would be furious at that. She went off by herself.'

'Gertrude must put up with it. She fits the rhetoric of

27

the occasion,' says the Abbess. She bends once more over her work. But the bell for Lauds chimes from the chapel. It is three in the morning. Faithful to the Rule, the Abbess immediately puts down her pen. One white swan, two black, they file from the room and down to the waiting hall. The whole congregation is assembled in steady composure. One by one they take their cloaks and follow the Abbess to the chapel, so softly ill-lit for Lauds. The nuns in their choirs chant and reply, with wakeful voices at three in the morning:

> *O Lord, our Lord, how wonderful*
> *is thy name in all the earth:*
>> *Thou who hast proclaimed thy*
>> *glory upon the heavens.*
> *Out of the mouths of babes and*
> *sucklings thou hast prepared praise*
> *to confuse thy adversaries:*
>> *to silence the enemy and the revengeful.*

The Abbess from her high seat looks with a kind of wonder at her shadowy chapel of nuns, she listens with a fine joy to the keen plainchant, as if upon a certain newly created world. She contemplates and sees it is good. Her lips move with the Latin of the psalm. She stands before her high chair as one exalted by what she sees and thinks, as it might be she is contemplating the full existence of the Abbess of Crewe.

> *Et fecisti eum paulo minorem Angelis:*
> *Gloria et honore coronasti eum.*

Soon she is whispering the melodious responses in other words of her great liking:

Every farthing of the cost,
All the dreaded cards foretell,
Shall be paid, but from this night
Not a whisper, not a thought,
Not a kiss nor look be lost.

curtains back to before election

Chapter 2

IN the summer before the autumn, as God is in his heaven, Sister Felicity's thimble is lying in its place in her sewing-box.

The Abbess Hildegarde is newly dead, and laid under her slab in the chapel.

The Abbey of Crewe is left without a head, but the election of the new Abbess is to take place in twenty-three days' time. After Matins, at twenty minutes past midnight, the nuns go to their cells to sleep briefly and deeply until their awakening for Lauds at three. But Felicity jumps from her window on to the haycart pulled up below and runs to meet her Jesuit.

Tall Alexandra, at this time Sub-Prioress and soon to be elected Abbess of Crewe, remains in the chapel, kneeling to pray at Hildegarde's tomb. She whispers:

> *Sleep on, my love, in thy cold bed*
> *Never to be disquieted.*
> *My last goodnight! Thou wilt not wake*
> *Till I thy fate shall overtake:*
> *Till age, or grief, or sickness must*
> *Marry my body to that dust*
> *It so much loves, and fill the room*
> *My heart keeps empty in thy tomb.*

She wears the same black habit as the two sisters who wait for her at the door of the chapel.

She joins them, and with their cloaks flying in the night air they return to the great sleeping house. Up and down the dark cloisters they pace, Alexandra, Walburga and Mildred.

'What are we here for?' says Alexandra. 'What are we doing here?'

'It's our destiny,' Mildred says.

'You will be elected Abbess, Alexandra,' says Walburga.

'And Felicity?'

'Her destiny is the Jesuit,' says Mildred.

'She has a following among the younger nuns,' Walburga says.

'It's a result of her nauseating propaganda,' says lofty Alexandra. 'She's always talking about love and freedom as if these were attributes peculiar to herself. Whereas, in reality, Felicity cannot love. How can she truly love? She's too timid to hate well, let alone love. It takes courage to practise love. And what does she know of freedom? Felicity has never been in bondage, bustling in, as she does, late for Mass, bleary-eyed for Prime, straggling vaguely through the Divine Office. One who has never observed a strict ordering of the heart can never exercise freedom.'

'She keeps her work-box tidy,' Mildred says. 'She's very particular about her work-box.'

'Felicity's sewing-box is the precise measure of her love and her freedom,' says Alexandra, so soon to be Abbess of Crewe. 'Her sewing-box is her alpha and her omega, not to mention her tiny epsilon, her iota and her omicron. For all her talk, and her mooney Jesuit and her pious eyelashes, it all adds up to Felicity's little sewing-box, the norm she departs from, the north of her compass. She would ruin the Abbey if she were elected. How strong is her following?'

'About as strong as she is weak. When it comes to the vote she'll lose,' Mildred says.

Walburga says sharply, 'This morning the polls put her at forty-two per cent according to my intelligence reports.'

'It's quite alarming,' says Alexandra, 'seeing that to be the Abbess of Crewe is my destiny.' She has stopped walking and the two nuns have stopped with her. She stands facing them, drawing their careful attention to herself, lighthouse that she is. 'Unless I fulfil my destiny my mother's labour pains were pointless and what am I doing here?'

'This morning the novices were talking about Felicity,' Mildred says. She was seen from their window wandering in the park between Lauds and Prime. They think she had a rendezvous.'

'Oh, well, the novices have no vote.'

'They reflect the opinions of the younger nuns.'

'Have you got a record of all this talk?'

'It's on tape,' says Mildred.

Walburga says, 'We must do something about it.' Walburga's face has a grey-green tinge; it is long and smooth. An Abbess needs must be over forty years, but Walburga, who has just turned forty, has no ambition but that Alexandra shall be elected and she remain the Prioress.

Walburga is strong; on taking her final vows she

brought to the community an endowment of a piece of London, this being a section of Park Lane with its view of Rotten Row, besides an adjoining mews of great value. Her strength resides in her virginity of heart combined with the long education of her youth that took her across many an English quad by night, across many a campus of Europe and so to bed. A wealthy woman, more than most, she has always maintained, is likely to remain virgin at heart. Her past lovers had been the most learned available; however ungainly, it was invariably the professors, the more profound scholars, who attracted her. And she always felt learned herself, thereafter, by a kind of osmosis.

Mildred, too, has brought a fortune to the Abbey. Her portion includes a sizeable block of Chicago slums in addition to the four big flats in the Boulevard St Germain. Mildred is thirty-six and would be too young to be a candidate for election, even if she were disposed to be Abbess. But her hopes, like Walburga's, rest on Alexandra. This Mildred has been in the convent since her late schooldays; it may be she is a nourisher of dreams so unrealizable in their magnitude that she prefers to keep them in mind and remain physically an inferior rather than take on any real fact of ambition that would defeat her. She has meekly served and risen to be Novice Mistress, so exemplary a nun with her blue eyes, her pretty face and nervous flutter of timidity that Thomas the Jesuit would at first have preferred to take her rather than Felicity. He had tried, following her from confession, waiting for her under the poplars.

'What did you confess?' he asked Mildred. 'What

33

did you say to that young priest? What are your sins?'

'It's between myself and God. It is a secret.'

'And the priest? What did you tell that young confessor of your secrets?'

'All my heart. It's necessary.'

He was jealous but he lost. Whatever Mildred's deeply concealed dreams might be, they ran far ahead of the Jesuit, far beyond him. He began at last to hate Mildred and took up with Felicity.

Alexandra, who brought to the community no dowry but her noble birth and shrewd spirit, is to be Abbess now that Hildegarde lies buried in the chapel. And the wonder is that she bothers, or even her favourite nuns are concerned, now, a few weeks before the election, that Felicity causes a slight stir amongst the forty nuns who are eligible to vote. Felicity has new and wild ideas and is becoming popular.

Under the late Abbess Hildegarde this quaint convent, quasi-Benedictine, quasi-Jesuit, has already discarded its quasi-natures. It is a mutation and an established fact. The Lady Abbess Hildegarde, enamoured of Alexandra as she was, came close to expelling Felicity from the Abbey in the days before she died. Alexandra alone possesses the authority and the means to rule. When it comes to the vote it needs must be Alexandra.

They pace the dark cloisters in such an evident happiness of shared anxiety that they seem not to recognize the pleasure at all.

Walburga says, 'We must do something. Felicity could create a crisis of leadership in the Abbey.'

'A crisis of leadership,' Mildred says, as one who enjoys both the phrase and the anguish of the idea. 'The community must be kept under the Rule, which is to say, Alexandra.'

Alexandra says, 'Keep watch on the popularity chart. Sisters, I am consumed by the Divine Discontent. We are made a little lower than the angels. This weighs upon me, because I am a true believer.'

'I too,' says Walburga. 'My faith remains firm.'

'And mine,' Mildred says. 'There was a time I greatly desired not to believe, but I found myself at last unable not to believe.'

Walburga says, 'And Felicity, your enemy, Ma'am? How is Felicity's faith. Does she really believe one damn thing about the Catholic faith?'

'She claims a special enlightenment,' says Alexandra the Abbess-to-be. 'Felicity wants everyone to be liberated by her vision and to acknowledge it. She wants a stamped receipt from Almighty God for every word she spends, every action, as if she can later deduct it from her income-tax returns. Felicity will never see the point of faith unless it visibly benefits mankind.'

'She is so bent on helping lame dogs over stiles,' Walburga says. 'Then they can't get back over again to limp home.'

'So it is with the Jesuit. Felicity is helping Thomas, she would say. I'm sure of it,' Mildred says. 'That was clear from the way he offered to help me.'

The Sisters walk hand in hand and they laugh, now, together in the dark night of the Abbey cloisters. Alexandra, between the two, skips as she walks and laughs at the idea that one of them might need help of the Jesuit.

The night-watch nun crosses the courtyard to ring the bell for Lauds. The three nuns enter the house. In the great hall a pillar seems to stir. It is Winifrede come to join them, with her round face in the moonlight, herself a zone of near-darkness knowing only that she has a serviceable place in the Abbey's hierarchy.

'Winifrede, *Benedicite*,' Alexandra says.

'*Deo Gratias*, Alexandra.'

'After Lauds we meet in the parlour,' Alexandra says.

'I've got news,' says Winifrede.

'Later, in the parlour,' says Walburga. And Mildred says, 'Not here, Winifrede!'

But Winifrede proceeds like beer from an unstoppered barrel. 'Felicity is lurking somewhere in the avenue. She was with Thomas the Jesuit. I have them on tape and on video-tape from the closed-circuit.'

Alexandra says, loud and clear, 'I don't know what rubbish you are talking.' And motions with her eyes to the four walls. Mildred whispers low to Winifrede, 'Nothing must be said in the hall. How many times have we told you?'

'Ah,' breathes Winifrede, aghast at her mistake. 'I forgot you've just bugged the hall.'

So swiftly to her forehead in despair goes the hand of Mildred, so swivelled to heaven are Walburga's eyes in the exasperation of the swifter mind with the slow. But Alexandra is calm. 'Order will come out of chaos,' she says, 'as it always has done. Sisters, be still, be sober.'

Walburga the Prioress turns to her: 'Alexandra, you are calm, so calm . . . '

'There is a proverb: Beware the ire of the calm,' says Alexandra.

Quietly the congregation of nuns descends the great staircase and is assembled. Walburga the Prioress now leads, Alexandra follows, and all the community after them, to sing the Hour.

It is the Hour of None, three in the afternoon, when Sister Felicity slips sleepily into the chapel. She is a tiny nun, small as a schoolgirl, not at all like what one would have imagined from all the talk about her. Her complexion looks as if her hair, sprouting under her veil, would be reddish. Nobody knows where Felicity has been all day and half the night, for she was not present at Matins at midnight nor Lauds at three in the morning, nor at breakfast at five, Prime at six, Terce at nine; nor was she present in the refectory at eleven for lunch, which comprised barley broth and a perfectly nourishing and tasty, although uncommon, dish of something unnamed on toast, that something being in fact a cat-food by the name of Mew, bought cheaply and in bulk. Felicity was not there to partake of it, nor was she in the chapel singing the Hour of Sext at noon. Nor between these occasions was she anywhere in the convent, not in her cell nor in the sewing-room embroidering the purses, the vestments and the altar-cloths; nor was she in the electronics laboratory which was set up by the great nuns Alexandra, Walburga and

37

Mildred under the late Abbess Hildegarde's very nose and carefully unregarding eyes. Felicity has been absent since after Vespers the previous day, and now she slips into her stall in the chapel at None, yawning at three in the afternoon.

Walburga, the Prioress, temporarily head of the convent, turns her head very slightly as Felicity takes her place, and turns away again. The community vibrates like an evanescent shadow that quickly fades out of sight, and continues fervently to sing. Puny Felicity, who knows the psalter by heart, takes up the chant but not her Office book:

They have spoken to me with a lying tongue and have compassed me about with words of hatred:
And have fought against me without cause.
Instead of making me a return of love, they slandered me:
but I gave myself to prayer.
And they repaid evil for good:
and hatred for my love.

The high throne of the Abbess is empty. Felicity's eyes, pink-rimmed with sleeplessness, turn towards it as she chants, thinking, maybe, of the dead, aloof Abbess Hildegarde who lately sat propped in that place, or maybe how well she could occupy it herself, little as she is, a life-force of new ideas, a quivering streak of light set in that gloomy chair. The late Hildegarde tolerated Felicity only because she considered her to be a common little thing, and it befitted a Christian to tolerate.

'She constitutes a reliable something for us to practise benevolence upon,' the late Hildegarde formerly said of Felicity, confiding this to Alexandra, Walburga and Mildred one summer afternoon between the Hours of Sext and None.

Felicity now looks away from the vacant throne and, intoning her responses, peers at Alexandra where she stands mightily in her stall. Alexandra's lips move with the incantation:

> *As I went down the water side,*
> *None but my foe to be my guide,*
> *None but my foe. . .*

Felicity, putting the finishing touches on an altar-cloth, is sewing a phrase into the inside corner. She is doing it in the tiniest and neatest possible satin-stitch, white upon white, having traced the words with her fine pencil: '*Opus Anglicanum*'. Her little frail fingers move securely and her silver thimble flashes.

The other sewing nuns are grouped around her, each busy with embroidery but none so clever at her work as Felicity.

'You know, Sisters,' Felicity says, 'our embroidery room is becoming known as a hotbed of sedition.'

The other nuns, eighteen in all, murmur solemnly. Felicity does not permit laughter. It is written in the Rule that laughter is unseemly. 'What are the tools of Good Works?' says the Rule, and the answers include, 'Not to say what is idle or causes laughter.' Of all the clauses of the Rule this is the one that Felicity decrees to be the least outmoded, the most adapted to the urgency of our times.

'Love,' says Felicity softly, plying her little fingers to

39

her satin-stitch, 'is lacking in our Community. We are full of prosperity. We prosper. We are materialistic. May God have mercy on our late Lady Abbess Hildegarde.'

'Amen,' say the other eighteen, and the sun of high summer dances on their thimbles through the window panes.

'Sometimes,' Felicity says, 'I think we should tend more towards the teachings of St Francis of Assisi, who understood total dispossession and love.'

One of her nuns, a certain Sister Bathildis, answers, her eyes still bent on her beautiful embroidery, 'But Sister Alexandra doesn't care for St Francis of Assisi.'

'Alexandra,' says Felicity 'has actually said, "To hell with St Francis of Assisi. I prefer Sextus Propertius who belongs also to Assisi, a contemporary of Jesus and a spiritual forerunner of Hamlet, Werther, Rousseau and Kierkegaard." According to Alexandra these fellows are far more interesting neurotics than St Francis. Have you ever heard of such names or such a doctrine?'

'Never,' murmur the nuns in unison, laying their work on their laps the easier to cross themselves.

'Love,' says Felicity as they all take up their work again, 'and love-making are very liberating experiences, very. If I were the Abbess of Crewe, we should have a love-Abbey. I would destroy that ungodly electronics laboratory and install a love-nest right in the heart of this Abbey, right in the heart of England.' Her busy little fingers fly with the tiny needle in and out of the stuff she is sewing.

'What do you make of that?' says Alexandra, switching off the closed-circuit television where she and her two trusted nuns have just witnessed the scene in the sewing-room, recorded on video and sound tape.

'It's the same old song,' Walburga says. 'It goes on all the time. More and more nuns are taking up embroidery of their own free will, and fewer and fewer remain with us. Since the Abbess died there is no more authority in the convent.'

'All that will be changed now,' Alexandra says, 'after the election.'

'It could be changed now,' Mildred says. 'Walburga is Prioress and has the authority.'

Walburga says, 'I thought better than to confront Felicity with her escapade last night and half of the day. I thought better of it, and I think better of preventing the nuns from joining the sewing-room faction. It might provoke Felicity to lead a rebellion.'

'Oh, do you think the deserters can have discovered that the convent is bugged?' says Mildred.

'Not on your life,' says Alexandra. 'The laboratory nuns are far too stupid to do anything but wire wires and screw screws. They have no idea at all what their work adds up to.'

They are sitting at the bare metal table in the private control room which was set up in the room adjoining the late Abbess's parlour shortly before her death. The parlour itself remains as it was when Hildegarde died although within a few weeks it will be changed to suit Alexandra's taste. For certainly Alexandra is to be Abbess of Crewe. And as surely, at this moment, the

41

matter has been thrown into doubt by Sister Felicity's glamorous campaign.

'She is bored,' says the destined Abbess. 'That is the trouble. She provides an unwholesome distraction for the nuns for a while, and after a while they will find her as boring as she actually is.'

'Gertrude,' says Alexandra into the green telephone. 'Gertrude, my dear, are you not returning to your convent for the election?'

'Impossible,' says Gertrude, who has been called on the new green line at the capital city nearest to that uncharted spot in the Andes where she has lately posted herself. 'I'm at a very delicate point in my negotiations between the cannibal tribe and that vegetarian sect on the other side of the mountain.'

'But, Gertrude, we're having a lot of trouble with Felicity. The life of the Abbey of Crewe is at stake, Gertrude.'

'The salvation of souls comes first,' says Gertrude's husky voice. 'The cannibals are to be converted to the faith with dietary concessions and the excessive zeal of the vegetarian heretics suppressed.'

'What puzzles me so much, Gertrude, my love, is how the cannibals will fare on the Day of Judgment,' Alexandra says cosily. 'Remember, Gertrude, that friendly little verse of our childhood:

> *It's a very odd thing —*
> *As odd as can be —*
> *That whatever Miss T. eats*
> *Turns into Miss T. . . .*

And it seems to me, Gertrude, that you are going to have a problem with those cannibals on the Latter Day when the trumpet shall sound. It's a question of which man shall rise in the Resurrection, for certainly those that are eaten have long since become the consumers from generation to generation. It is a problem, Gertrude, my most clever angel, that vexes my noon's repose and I do urge you to leave well alone in that field. You should come back at once to Crewe and help us in our time of need.'

Something crackles on the line. 'Gertrude, are you there?' says Alexandra.

Something crackles, then Gertrude's voice responds, 'Sorry, I missed all that. I was tying my shoelace.'

'You should be here, Gertrude. The nuns are beginning to murmur that you're avoiding us. Felicity is saying that if she's elected Abbess of Crewe she wants an open audit of all the dowries and she advocates indiscreet sex. Above all, she has proclaimed a rebellion in the house and it's immoral.'

'What is her rebellion against?' Gertrude inquires.

'My tyranny,' says Alexandra. 'What do you think?'

'Is the rebellion likely to succeed?' says Gertrude.

'Not if we can help it. But she has a chance. Her following increases every hour.'

'If she has a chance of success then the rebellion isn't immoral. A rebellion against a tyrant is only immoral when it hasn't got a chance.'

'That sounds very cynical, Gertrude. Positively

Machiavellian. Don't you think it a little daring to commit yourself so far?'

'It is the doctrine of St Thomas Aquinas.'

'Can you be here for the election, Gertrude? We need to consult you.'

'Consult Machiavelli,' says Gertrude. 'A great master, but don't quote me as saying so; the name is inexpedient.'

'Gertrude,' says Alexandra. 'Do bear in mind that

> *Tiny and cheerful,*
> *And neat as can be,*
> *Whatever Miss T. eats*
> *Turns into Miss T.'*

But Gertrude has hung up.

'Will she come home?' says Walburga when Alexandra turns from the telephone.

'I doubt it,' says Alexandra. 'She is having a great success with the cannibals and has administered the Kiss of Peace according to the photograph in today's *Daily Mirror*. Meanwhile the vegetarian tribes have guaranteed to annihilate the cannibals, should they display any desire to roast her.'

'She will be in trouble with Rome,' says Mildred, 'if she absents herself from the Abbey much longer. A mission takes so long and no longer according to the vows of this Abbey.'

'Gertrude fears neither Pope nor man,' says Alexandra. 'Call Sister Winifrede on the walkie-talkie. Tell Winifrede to come to the Abbess's parlour.' She leads the way into the parlour which is still furnished in

44

the style of the late Hildegarde, who had a passion for autumn tints. The carpet is figured with fallen leaves and the wallpaper is a faded glow of browns and golds. The three nuns recline in the greenish-brown plush chairs while Winifrede is summoned and presently appears before them, newly startled out of a snooze.

Alexandra, so soon to be clothed in white, fetches from her black pocket a bunch of keys. 'Winifrede,' she says, indicating one of the keys, 'this is the key to the private library. Open it up and bring me Machiavelli's *Art of War*.' Alexandra then selects another key. 'And while you are about it go to my cell and open my locked cupboard. In it you will find my jar of *pâté*, some fine little biscuits and a bottle of my *Le Corton*, 1959. Prepare a tray for four and bring it here with the book.'

'Alexandra,' whines Winifrede, 'why not get one of the kitchen nuns to prepare the tray?'

'On no account,' says Alexandra. 'Do it yourself. You'll get your share.'

'The kitchen nuns are so ugly,' says Mildred.

'And such common little beasts,' says Walburga.

'Very true,' says Winifrede agreeably and departs on her errands.

'Winifrede is useful,' says Alexandra.

'We can always make use of Winifrede,' says Mildred.

'Highly dependable,' says Walburga. 'She'll come in useful when we really come to grips with Felicity.'

'That, of course, is for you two nuns to decide,' Alexandra says. 'As a highly obvious candidate for the

45

Abbey of Crewe, plainly I can take no personal part in whatever you have in mind.'

'Really, I have nothing in mind,' Mildred says.

'Nor I,' says Walburga. 'Not as yet.'

'It will come to you,' says Alexandra. 'I see no reason why I shouldn't start now arranging for this room to be newly done over. A green theme, I think. I'm attached to green. An idea of how to proceed against Felicity will occur to you quite soon, I imagine, tomorrow or the day after, between the hours of Matins and Lauds, or Lauds and Prime, or Prime and Terce, or, maybe, between Terce and Sext, Sext and Nonc, None and Vespers, or between Vespers and Compline.' Winifrede returns, tall and handsome as a transvested butler, bearing a tray laden with their private snack for four. She sets it on a table and, fishing into her pocket, produces a book and Alexandra's keys which she hands over.

They are seated at the table, and the wine is poured. 'Shall I say grace?' says fair-faced, round-eyed Winifrede, although the others have already started to scoop daintily at the *pâté* with their pearl-handled knives. 'Oh, it isn't necessary,' says Alexandra, spreading the *pâté* on her fine wafer, 'there's nothing wrong with *my* food.'

Winifrede, with her eyes like two capital Os, leans forward and confides, 'I've seen the print of that telephoto of Felicity with Thomas this morning.'

'I, too,' says Walburga. 'I don't understand these fresh-air fiends when the traditional linen cupboard is so much better heated and equipped.'

Alexandra says, 'I glanced at the negative. Since

46

when my spirit is impure. It does not become them. Only the beautiful should make love when they are likely to be photographed.'

'The double monasteries of the olden days were so discreet and so well ordered,' Mildred says, wistfully.

'I intend to reinstate the system,' says Alexandra. 'If I am the Abbess of Crewe for a few years I shall see to it that each nun has her own private chaplain, as in the days of my ancestor St Gilbert, Rector of Sempringham. The nuns will have each her Jesuit. The lay brothers, who will take the place of domestic nuns as in the eleventh century, will be Cistercians, which is to say, bound to silence. Now, if you please, Walburga, let's consult *The Art of War* because time is passing and the sands are running out.'

Alexandra gracefully pushes back her plate and leans in her chair, one elbow resting on the back of it and her long body arranged the better to finger through the pages of the book placed on the table before her. The white coifs meet in a tent of concentration above the book where Alexandra's fingers trace the passages to be well noted.

'It is written,' says Alexandra with her lovely index finger on the margin as she reads:

After you have consulted many about what you ought to do, confer with very few concerning what you are actually resolved to do.

The bell rings for Matins, and Alexandra closes the book. Walburga leads the way while Alexandra counsels them, 'Sisters, be vigilant, be sober. This is a monastery under threat, and we must pray to Almighty God for our strength.'

'We can't do more,' says Mildred.

'To do less would be cheap,' Walburga says.

'We are corrupt by our nature in the Fall of Man,' Alexandra says. 'It was well exclaimed by St Augustine, "O happy fault to merit such a Redeemer! *O felix culpa!*" '

'Amen,' respond the three companions.

They start to descend the stairs. 'O happy flaw!' says Alexandra.

Felicity is already waiting with her assembled supporters and the anonymous files of dark-shaped nuns when the three descend, graceful with Walburga in the lead, each one of them so nobly made and well put together. One by one they take their capes and file across the midnight path to their chapel.

Felicity slips aside, waiting with her cloak folded in the dark air until the community has entered the chapel. Then, while the voices start to sound in the ebb and flow of the plainchant, she makes her way back across the grass to the house quickly as a water bird skimming a pond. Felicity is up the great staircase, she is in the Abbess's parlour and switches on the light. Her little face looks at the remains of the little feast; she spits at it like an exasperated beggar-gipsy, and she breathes a cat's hiss to see such luxury spent. But soon she is about her business, through the door, and is occupied with the apparatus of the green telephone.

At the end of a long ring someone answers.

'Gertrude!' she says. 'Can that really be you?'

'I was just about to leave,' Gertrude says. 'The helicopter is waiting.'

'Gertrude, you're doing such marvellous work. We hear – '

'Is that all you want to say?' Gertrude says.

'Gertrude, this convent is a hotbed of corruption and hypocrisy. I want to change everything and a lot of the nuns agree with me. We want to break free. We want justice.'

'Sister, be still, be sober,' Gertrude says. 'Justice may be done but on no account should it be seen to be done. It's always a fatal undertaking. You'll bring down the whole community in ruins.'

'Oh, Gertrude, we believe in love in freedom and freedom in love.'

'That can be arranged,' Gertrude says.

'But I have a man in my life now, Gertrude. What can a poor nun do with a man?'

'Invariably, a man you feed both ends,' Gertrude says. 'You have to learn to cook and to do the other.'

The telephone then roars like a wild beast.

'What's going on, Gertrude?'

'The helicopter,' Gertrude says, and hangs up.

'Read it aloud to them,' Alexandra says. Once more it is lunch time. 'Let it never be said that we concealed our intentions. Our nuns are too bemused to take it in and those who are for Felicity have gone morbid with their sentimental Jesusism. Let it be read aloud. If they have ears to hear, let them hear.' The kitchen nuns float with their trays along the aisles between the

49

refectory tables, dispensing sieved nettles and mashed potatoes.

Winifrede stands at the lectern. She starts to read, announcing Ecclesiasticus, chapter 34, verse 1:

Fools are cheated by vain hopes, buoyed up with the fancies of a dream. Wouldst thou heed such lying visions? Better clutch at shadows, or chase the wind. Nought thou seest in a dream but symbols; man is but face to face with his own image. As well may foul thing cleanse, as false thing give thee a true warning. Out upon the folly of them, pretended divination, and cheating omen, and wizard's dream! Heart of woman in her pangs is not more fanciful. Unless it be some manifestation the most High has sent thee, pay no heed to any such; trust in dreams has crazed the wits of many, and brought them to their ruin. Believe rather the law's promises, that cannot miss their fulfilment, the wisdom that trusty counsellors shall make clear to thee.

Winifrede stops to turn the pages to the next place marked with a book-marker elaborately embroidered from the sewing-room. Her eyes remotely sweep the length of the room, where the kitchen nuns are bearing jugs up the aisles, pouring water which has been heated for encouragement into the nuns' beakers. The forks move to the faces and the mouths open to receive the food. These are all the nuns in the convent, with the exception of kitchen nuns and the novices who do not count and the senior nuns who do. A less edifying crowd of human life it would be difficult to find; either they have become so or they always were so; at any rate, they are in fact a very poor lot, all the more since they do not think so for a moment. Up pop the forks, open go the mouths, in slide the nettles and the potato mash. They raise to their frightful little lips the steaming beakers of water and they sip as if fancying they are partaking of the warm sap of human experience, ripe for Felicity's liberation. Anyway, the good Winifrede reads on, announcing Ecclesiastes, chapter 9, verse 11. 'Sisters, hear again,' she says, 'the wise confessions of Solomon':

Then my thought took a fresh turn; man's art does not avail, here beneath the sun, to win the race for the swift, or the battle for the strong, a livelihood for wisdom, riches for great learning, or for the craftsman thanks; chance and the moment rule all.

The kitchen staff is gliding alongside the tables now, removing the empty plates and replacing them with saucers of wholesome and filling sponge pudding which many more deserving cases than the nuns would be glad of. Winifrede sips from her own glass of water, which is cold, puts it down and bends her eyes to the next book marked with its elaborate markers, passage by passage, which she exchanges with the good book on her lectern. She dutifully removes a slip of paper from the inside cover and almost intelligent-looking in this company reads it aloud in her ever-keening voice: 'Further words of wisdom from one of our Faith':

If you suspect any person in your army of giving the enemy intelligence of your designs, you cannot do better than avail yourself of his treachery, by seeming to trust him with some secret resolution which you intend to execute, whilst you carefully conceal your real design; by which, perhaps, you may discover the traitor, and lead the enemy into an error that may possibly end in their destruction . . .

In order to penetrate into the secret designs, and discover the condition of an enemy, some have sent ambassadors to them with skilful and experienced officers in their train, dressed like the rest of their attendants . . .

As to private discords amongst your soldiers, the only remedy is to expose them to some danger, for in such cases fear generally unites them . . .

'Here endeth the reading,' Winifrede says, looking stupidly round the still more stupid assembly into whose ears the words have come and from which they have gone. The meal over, the nuns' hands are folded.

'Amen,' they say.

'Sisters, be vigilant, be sober.'

'Amen.'

Alexandra sits in the downstairs parlour where visitors are generally received. She has laid aside the copy of *The Discourses* of Machiavelli which she has been reading while awaiting the arrival of her two clergymen friends; these are now ushered in, accompanied by Mildred and Walburga.

Splendid Alexandra rises and stands, quiet and still, while they approach. It is Walburga, on account of being the Prioress, who asks the company to be seated.

'Father Jesuits,' says Walburga, 'our Sister Alexandra will speak.'

It is summer outside, and some of the old-fashioned petticoat roses that climb the walls of the Abbey look into the window at the scene, where Alexandra sits, one arm resting on the table, her head pensively inclining towards it. The self-controlled English sun makes leafy shadows fall on this polished table and across the floor. A bee importunes at the window-pane. The parlour is cool and fresh. A working nun can be seen outside labouring along with two pails, one of them probably unnecessary; and all things keep time with the season.

Walburga sits apart, smiling a little for sociability, with her eye on the door wherein soon enters the tray of afternoon tea, so premeditated in every delicious particular as to make the nun who bears it, leaves it, and goes away less noteworthy than ever.

The two men accept the cups of tea, the plates and the little lace-edged napkins from the sewing-room which Mildred takes over to them. They choose from among the cress sandwiches, the golden shortbread and the pastel-coloured *petit fours*. Both men are grey-haired, of about the same middle age as the three nuns. Alexandra refuses tea with a mannerly inclination of her body from the waist. These Jesuits are her friends. Father Baudouin is big and over-heavy with a face full of high blood-pressure; his companion, Father Maximilian, is more handsome, classic-featured and grave. They watch Alexandra attentively as her words fall in with the silvery acoustics of the tea-spoons.

'Fathers, there are vast populations in the world which are dying or doomed to die through famine, under-nourishment and disease; people continue to make war, and will not stop, but rather prefer to send their young children into battle to be maimed or to die; political fanatics terrorize indiscriminately; tyrannous states are overthrown and replaced by worse tyrannies; the human race is possessed of a universal dementia; and it is at such a moment as this, Fathers, that your brother-Jesuit Thomas has taken to screwing our Sister Felicity by night under the poplars, so that her mind is given over to nothing else but to induce our nuns to follow her example in the name of freedom. They thought they had liberty till Felicity told them they had not. And now she aspires to bear the crozier of the Abbess of Crewe. Fathers, I suggest you discuss this scandal and what you propose to do about it with my two Sisters, because it is beyond me and beneath me.'

Alexandra rises and goes to the door, moving like a Maharajah aloft on his elephant. The Jesuits seem distressed.

'Sister Alexandra,' says the larger Jesuit, Baudouin, as he opens the door for her, 'you know there's very little we can do about Thomas. Alexandra – '

'Then do that very little,' she says in the voice of one whose longanimity foreshortens like shadows cast by the poplars amid the blaze of noon.

Fathers Baudouin and Maximilian will sit late into the night conferring with Mildred and Walburga.

'Mildred,' says handsome Maximilian, 'I know you can be counted on to be tough with the nuns.'

That Mildred the Novice Mistress is reliably tough with the lesser nuns is her only reason for being so closely in Alexandra's confidence. Her mind sometimes wavers with little gusts of timidity when she is in the small environment of her equals. She shivers now as Maximilian addresses her with a smile of confidence.

Baudouin looks from Mildred's heart-shaped white face to Walburga's strong dark face, two portraits in matching white frames. 'Sisters,' Baudouin says, 'Felicity ought not to be the Abbess of Crewe.'

'It must be Alexandra,' Walburga says.

'It shall be Alexandra,' says Mildred.

'Then we have to discuss an assault strategy in dealing with Felicity,' says Baudouin.

'We could deal with Felicity very well,' Walburga says, 'if you would deal with Thomas.'

'The two factors are one,' Maximilian says, smiling wistfully at Mildred.

The bell rings for Vespers. Walburga, looking straight ahead, says, 'We shall have to miss Vespers.'

'We'll miss all the Hours until we've got a plan,' Mildred says decisively.

'And Alexandra?' says Baudouin. 'Won't Alexandra return to join us? We should consult Alexandra.'

'Certainly not, Fathers,' Walburga says. 'She will not join us and we may not consult her. It would be dishonourable – '

'Seeing she is likely to be Abbess,' says Mildred.

'Seeing she will be Abbess,' Walburga says.

55

'Well, it seems to me that you girls are doing plenty of campaigning,' Baudouin says, looking round the room uncomfortably, as if some fresh air were missing.

Maximilian says, 'Baudouin!' and the nuns look down, offended, at their empty hands in their lap.

After a space, Mildred says, 'We may not canvass for votes. It is against the Rule.'

'I see, I see,' says large Baudouin, patiently.

They talk until Vespers are over and the black shape comes in to remove the tea tray. Still they talk on, and Mildred calls for supper. The priests are shown to the visitors' cloakroom and Mildred retires with Walburga to the upstairs lavatories where they exchange a few words of happiness. The plans are going well and are going forward.

The four gather again, conspiring over a good supper with wine. The bell rings for Compline, and they talk on.

Upstairs and far away in the control room the recorders, activated by their voices, continue to whirl. So very much elsewhere in the establishment do the walls have ears that neither Mildred nor Walburga are now conscious of them as they were when the mechanisms were first installed. It is like being told, and all the time knowing, that the Eyes of God are upon us; it means everything and therefore nothing. The two nuns speak as freely as the Jesuits who suspect no eavesdropping device more innocuous than God to be making a chronicle of their present privacy.

The plainchant of Compline floats sweetly over from the chapel where Alexandra stands in her stall nearly opposite Felicity. Walburga's place is empty, Mildred's place is empty. In the Abbess's chair, not quite an emptiness as yet, but the absence of Hildegarde.

The voices ripple like a brook:

> *Hear, O God, my supplication:*
> *be attentive to my prayers.*
> *From the ends of the earth I cry to thee:*
> *when my heart fails me.*
> *Thou wilt set me high upon a rock, thou wilt*
> *give me rest:*
> *thou art my fortress, a tower of strength against*
> *the face of the enemy.*

And Alexandra's eyes grieve, her lips recite:

> *For I am homesick after mine own kind*
> *And ordinary people touch me not.*
>   *And I am homesick*
> *After my own kind . . .*

Winifrede, taking over Mildred's duty, is chanting in true tones the short lesson to Felicity's clear responses:

> *Sisters: Be sober and vigilant:*
> *for thy enemy the devil, as a raging lion, goeth about*
> *seeking whom he may devour. Him do thou resist . . .*

'Aye, I am wistful for my kin of the spirit'; softly flows the English verse beloved of Alexandra:

57

Well then, so call they, the swirlers out of the mist of my
    soul,
They that come mewards, bearing old magic.

But for all that, I am homesick after mine own kind . . .

Chapter 3

FELICITY'S work-box is known as Felicity's only because she brought it to the convent as part of her dowry. It is no mean box, being set on fine tapered legs with castors, standing two and a half feet high. The box is inlaid with mother-of-pearl and inside it has three tiers neatly set out with needles, scissors, cottons and silks in perfect compartments. Beneath all these is a false bottom lined with red watered silk, for love-letters. Many a time has Alexandra stood gazing at this box with that certain wonder of the aristocrat at the treasured toys of the bourgeoisie. 'I fail to see what mitigation soever can be offered for that box,' she remarked one day, in Felicity's hearing, to the late Abbess Hildegarde who happened to be inspecting the sewing-room. Hildegarde made no immediate reply, but once outside the room she said, 'It is in poison-bad taste, but we are obliged by our vows to accept mortifications. And, after all, everything is hidden here. Nobody but ourselves can see what is beautiful and what is not.'

Hildegarde's dark eyes, now closed in death, gazed at Alexandra. 'Even our beauty,' she said, 'may not be thought of.'

'What should we care,' said Alexandra, 'about our beauty, since we are beautiful, you and I, whether we care or not?'

Meanwhile Felicity, aggrieved, regarded her work-box and opened it to see that all was in order. So she does every morning and by custom, now, she once more strokes the elaborate shining top after the Hour of Prime while the ordinary nuns, grown despicable by profession, file in to the sewing-room and take their places.

Felicity opens the box. She surveys the neat compartments, the reels and the skeins, the needles and the little hooks. Suddenly she gives a short scream and with her tiny bad-tempered face looking round the room at everybody she says, 'Who has touched my work-box?'

There is no answer. The nuns have come all unprepared for a burst of anger. The day of the election is not far off. The nuns have come in full expectance of Felicity's revelations about the meaningful life of love as it should be lived on the verge of the long walk lined with poplars.

Felicity now speaks with a low and strained voice. 'My box is disarranged. My thimble is missing.' Slowly she lifts the top layer and surveys the second. 'It has been touched,' she says. She raises the lowest recess and looks inside. She decides, then, to empty the work-box the better to examine the contents of its secret compartment.

'Sisters,' she says, 'I think my letters have been discovered.'

It is like a wind rushing over a lake with a shudder of birds and reeds. Felicity counts the letters. 'They are all here,' she says, 'but they have been looked at. My thimble is lost. I can't find it.'

Everyone looks for Felicity's thimble. Nobody finds it. The bell goes for the Hour of Terce. The first part of the morning has been a sheer waste of sensation and the nuns file out to their prayers, displaying, in their discontent, a trace of individualism at long last.

How gentle is Alexandra when she hears of Felicity's distress! 'Be gentle with her,' she tells the senior nuns. 'Plainly she is undergoing a nervous crisis. A thimble after all – a thimble. I wouldn't be surprised if she has not herself, in a moment of unconscious desire to pitch all her obsessive needlework to hell and run away with her lover, mislaid the ridiculous thimble. Be gentle. It is beautiful to be gentle with those who suffer. There is no beauty in the world so great as beauty of action. It stands, contained in its own moment, from everlasting to everlasting.'

Winifrede, cloudily recognizing the very truth of Alexandra's words, is yet uncertain what reason Alexandra might have for uttering them at this moment. Walburga and Mildred stand silently in the contemplative hush while Alexandra leaves them to continue their contemplations. For certainly Alexandra means what she says, not wishing her spirit to lose serenity before God nor her destiny to be the Abbess of Crewe. Very soon the whole community has been informed of these thoughts of the noble Alexandra and marvel a little that, with the election so close at hand, she exhorts gentleness towards her militant rival.

Felicity's rage all the next day shakes her little body to shrieking point. There is a plot, there is a plot,

61

against me, is the main theme of all she says to her sewing companions between the Hours of Lauds and Prime, Prime and Terce, Terce and Sext. In the afternoon, she takes to her bed, while her bewildered friends hunt the thimble and are well overheard in the control room in all their various exchanges and conjectures.

Towards evening Walburga reports to Alexandra, 'Her supporters are wavering. The nasty little bitch can't stand our gentleness.'

'You know, Walburga,' Alexandra muses, 'from this moment on, you may not report such things to me. Everything now is in your hands and those of Sister Mildred; you are together with Fathers Baudouin and Maximilian, and you are with the aid of Winifrede. I must remain in the region of unknowing. Proceed but don't tell me. I refuse to be told, such knowledge would not become me; I am to be the Abbess of Crewe, not a programmed computer.'

Felicity lies on her hard bed and at the midnight bell she rises for Matins. My God, there is a moving light in the sewing-room window! Felicity slips out of the file of black-cloaked nuns who make their hushed progress to the chapel. Alexandra leads. Walburga and Mildred are absent. There is a light in the sewing-room, moving as if someone is holding an electric torch.

The nuns are assembled in the chapel but Felicity stands on the lawn, gazing upward, and eventually she creeps back to the house and up the stairs.

So it is that she comes upon the two young men rifling her work-box. They have found the secret compartment. One of the young men holds in his hand

Felicity's love-letters. Screaming, Felicity retreats, locks the door with the intruders inside, runs to the telephone and calls the police.

In the control room, Mildred and Walburga are tuned in to the dim-lit closed-circuit television. 'Come quickly,' says Walburga to Mildred, 'follow me to the chapel. We must be seen at Matins.' Mildred trembles. Walburga walks firmly.

The bell clangs at the gate, but the nuns chant steadily. The police sirens sound in the drive, their car having been admitted by Felicity, but the Sisters continue the night's devotions:

> *He turned rivers into a desert:*
> *and springs of water into parched ground,*
> *A fruitful land into a salt waste:*
> *because of the wickedness of those who*
> *dwelt therein.*
> *He turned a desert into a pool of water:*
> *and an arid land into springs of water.*
> *And there he settled the hungry:*
> *and they founded a city to dwell in.*

Alexandra hears the clamour outside.

Sisters, be sober, be vigilant, for the devil as a raging lion . . .

The nuns file up to bed, anxiously whispering. Their heads bend meekly but their eyes have slid to right and to left where in the great hall the policemen stand with the two young men, dressed roughly, who have been caught in the convent. Felicity's voice comes in spasmodic gasps. She is recounting her story while her closest friend Bathildis holds her shaking body. Down upon them bear Walburga and Alexandra, swishing their habits with authority. Mildred motions the nuns upward and upward to their cells out of sight, far out of sight. Alexandra can be heard: 'Come into the parlour, sirs. Sister Felicity, be still, be sober.'

'Pull yourself together, Felicity,' Walburga says.

As the last nun reaches the last flight of stairs Winifrede in her handsome stupor comes out of the dark cupboard in the sewing-room and descends.

And, as it comes to pass, these men are discovered to be young Jesuit novices. In the parlour, they admit as much, and the police take notes.

'Officer,' says Walburga. 'I think this is merely a case of high spirits.'

'Some kind of a lark,' Alexandra says with an exalted and careless air. 'We have no charge to bring against them. We don't want a scandal.'

'Leave it to us,' says Walburga. 'We shall speak to their Jesuit superiors. No doubt they will be expelled from their Order.'

Sister Felicity screams, 'I bring a charge. They were here last night and they stole my thimble.'

'Well, Sister . . .' says the officer in charge, and gives a little grunt.

'It was a theft,' says Felicity.

The officer says, 'A thimble, ma'am, isn't much of a crime. Maybe you just mislaid it.' And he looks wistfully into the mother-of-pearl face of Alexandra, hoping for her support. These policemen, three of them, are very uneasy.

Young Bathildis says, 'It isn't only her thimble. They wanted some documents belonging to Sister Felicity.'

'In this covent we have no private property,' Walburga says. 'I am the Prioress, officer. So far as I'm concerned the incident is closed, and we're sorry you've been troubled.'

Felicity weeps loudly and is led from the room by Bathildis, who says vulgarly, 'It was a put-up job.'

In this way the incident is closed, and the two Jesuit novices cautioned, and the police implored by lovely Alexandra to respect the holiness of the nuns' cloistered lives by refraining from making a scandal. Respectfully the policemen withdraw, standing by with due reverence while Walburga, Alexandra and Mildred lead the way from the parlour.

Outside the door stands Winifrede. 'What a bungle!' she says.

'Nonsense,' says Walburga quickly. 'Our good friends, these officers here, have bungled nothing. They understand perfectly.'

'Young people these days, Sisters . . .' says the elder policeman.

They put the two young Jesuits in a police car to take them back to their seminary. As quietly as they can possibly go, they go.

Only a small piece appears in one of the daily papers, and then only in the first edition. Even so, Alexandra's

65

cousins, Walburga's sisters and Mildred's considerable family connections, without the slightest prompting, and not even troubling to question the fact, weigh in with quiet ferocity to protect their injured family nuns. First on the telephone and then, softly, mildly, in the seclusion of a men's club and the demure drawing-room of a great house these staunch families privately and potently object to the little newspaper story which is entitled 'Jesuit Novices on the Spree'. A Catholic spokesman is fabricated from the clouds of nowhere to be quoted by all to the effect that the story is a gross exaggeration, that it is ungallant, that it bears the heavy mark of religious prejudice and that really these sweet nuns should not be maligned. These nuns, it is pointed out, after all do not have the right of reply, and this claim, never demonstrated, is the most effective of all arguments. Anyway, the story fades into almost nothing; it is only a newspaper clipping lying on Alexandra's little desk. 'Jesuit Novices on the Spree', and a few merry paragraphs of how two student Jesuits gate-crashed the enclosed Abbey of Crewe and stole a nun's thimble. 'They did it for a bet,' explained Father Baudouin, assistant head of the Jesuit College. Denying that the police were involved, Father Baudouin stated that the incident was closed.

'Why in hell,' demands Alexandra, in the presence of Winifrede, Walburga and Mildred, 'did they take her thimble?'

'They broke in twice,' Winifrede says in her monotone of lament. 'The night before they were caught and the night they were caught. They came first to survey the scene and test the facility of entry, and they took

66

the thimble as a proof they'd done so. Fathers Baudouin and Maximilian were satisfied and therefore they came next night for the love-letters. It was –'

'Winifrede, let's hear no more,' Walburga says. 'Alexandra is to be innocent of the details. No specific items, please.'

'Well,' says obstinate Winifrede, 'she was just asking why the hell – '

'Alexandra has said no such thing,' Walburga menaces. 'She said nothing of the kind,' Mildred agrees.

Alexandra sits at her little desk and smiles.

'Alexandra, I heard it with my own ears. You were inquiring as to the thimble.'

'If you believe your own ears more than you believe us, Winifrede,' says Alexandra, 'then perhaps it is time for us to part. It may be you have lost your religious vocation, and we shall all quite understand if you decide to return to the world quietly, before the election.'

Dawn breaks for a moment through the terribly bad weather of Winifrede's understanding. She says, 'Sister Alexandra, you asked me for no explanation whatsoever, and I have furnished none.'

'Excellent,' says Alexandra. 'I love you so dearly, Winifrede, that I could eat you were it not for the fact that I can't bear suet pudding. Would you mind going away now and start giving all the nuns a piece of your mind. They are whispering and carrying on about the episode. Put Felicity under a three days' silence. Give her a new thimble and ten yards of poplin to hem.'

'Felicity is in the orchard with Thomas,' states Winifrede.

'Alexandra has a bad cold and her hearing is affected,' Walburga observes, looking at her pretty fingernails.

'Clear off,' says Mildred, which Winifrede does, and faithfully, meanwhile, the little cylindrical ears in the walls transmit the encounter; the tape-recorder receives it in the control room where spools, spools and spools twirl obediently for hours and many hours.

When Winifrede has gone, the three Sisters sit for a moment in silence, Alexandra regarding the press cutting, Walburga and Mildred regarding Alexandra.

'Felicity is in the orchard with Thomas,' Alexandra says, 'and she hopes to be Abbess of Crewe.'

'We have no video connection with the orchard,' says Mildred, 'not as yet.'

'Gertrude,' says Alexandra on the green telephone, 'we have news that you've crossed the Himalayas and are preaching birth-control. The Bishops are demanding an explanation. We'll be in trouble with Rome, Gertrude, my dear, and it's very embarrassing with the election so near.'

'I was only preaching to the birds like St Francis,' Gertrude says.

'Gertrude, where are you speaking from?'

'It's unpronounceable and they're changing the name of the town tomorrow to something equally unpronounceable.'

'We've had our difficulties here at Crewe,' says Alexandra. 'You had better come home, Gertrude, and assist with the election.'

'One may not canvass the election of an Abbess,' Gertrude says in her deepest voice. 'Each vote is a matter of conscience. Winifrede is to vote for me by proxy.'

'A couple of Jesuit novices broke into the convent during Compline and Felicity is going round the house saying they were looking for evidence against her. They took her thimble. She's behaving in a most menopausal way, and she claims there's a plot against her to prevent her being elected Abbess. Of course, it's a lot of nonsense. Why don't you come home, Gertrude, and make a speech about it?'

'I wasn't there at the time,' Gertrude says. 'I was here.'

'Have you got bronchitis, Gertrude?'

'No,' says Gertrude, 'you'd better make a speech yourself. Be careful not to canvass for votes.'

'Gertrude, my love, how do I go about appealing to these nuns' higher instincts? Felicity has disrupted their minds.'

'Appeal to their lower instincts,' Gertrude says, 'within the walls of the convent. It's only when exhorting the strangers outside that one appeals to the higher. I hear a bell at your end, Alexandra. I hear a lovable bell.'

'It's the bell for Terce,' Alexandra says. 'Are you not homesick, Gertrude, after your own kind?'

But Gertrude has rung off.

The nuns are assembled in the great chapter hall and

the Prioress Walburga addresses them. The nuns are arranged in semicircles according to their degree, with the older nuns at the back, the lesser and more despised in the middle rows and the novices in the front. Walburga stands on a dais at a table facing them, with the most senior nuns on either side of her. These comprise Felicity, Winifrede, Mildred and Alexandra.

'Sisters, be still, be sober,' says Walburga.

The nuns are fidgeting, however, in a way that has never happened before. The faces glance and the eyes dart as if they were at the theatre waiting for the curtain to go up, having paid for their tickets. Outside the rain pelts down on the green, on the gravel, on the spreading leaves; and inside the nuns rustle as if a small tempest were swelling up amongst them.

'Be sober, be vigilant,' says Walburga the Prioress, 'for I have asked Sister Alexandra to speak to you on the subject of our recent disturbances.'

Alexandra rises and bows to Walburga. She stands like a lightning-conductor, elegant in her black robes, so soon to be more radiant in white. 'Sisters, be still. I have first a message from our esteemed Sister Gertrude. Sister Gertrude is at present settling a dispute between two sects who reside beyond the Himalayas. The dispute is on a point of doctrine which apparently has arisen from a mere spelling mistake in English. True to her bold custom, Sister Gertrude has refused to furnish Rome with the tiresome details of the squabble and bloodshed in that area and she is settling it herself out of court. In the midst of these pressing affairs Sister Gertrude has found time to think of our recent trifling upset here at cosy Crewe, and she begs us to appeal to your higher instincts and wider vision, which is what I am about to do.'

The nuns are already sobered and made vigilant by the invocation of famous Gertrude, but Felicity on the dais causes a nervous distraction by bringing out from some big pocket under her black scapular a little embroidery frame. Felicity's fingers busy themselves with some extra flourish while Alexandra, having swept her eyes upon this frail exhibition, proceeds.

'Sisters,' she says, 'let me do as Sister Gertrude wishes; let me appeal to your higher instincts. We had the extraordinary experience, last week, of an intrusion into our midst, at midnight, of two young ruffians. It's natural that you should be distressed, and we know that you have been induced to gossip amongst yourselves about the incident, stories of which have been circulated outside the convent walls.'

Felicity's fingers fly to and fro; her eyes are downcast with pale, devout lashes, and she holds her sewing well up to meet them.

'Now,' says Alexandra, 'I am not here before you to speak of the ephemera of every day or of things that are of no account, material things that will pass and will become, as the poet says,

The love-tales wrought with silken thread
By dreaming ladies upon cloth
That has made fat the murderous moth ...

I call rather to the attention of your higher instincts the enduring tradition of one belonging to my own ancestral lineage, Marguerite Marie Alacoque of the seventeenth century, my illustrious aunt, founder of the great Abbeys of the Sacré Cœur. Let me remind you now of your good fortune, for in those days, you must know, the nuns were rigidly divided in two parts, the *sœurs nobles* and the *sœurs bourgeoises*. Apart from this distinction between the nobility and the bourgeoisie, there was of course a third section of the convent comprising the lay sisters who hardly count. Indeed, well into this century the Abbey schools of the Continent were divided; the *filles nobles* were taught by nuns of noble lineage while *sœurs bourgeoises* taught the daughters of the *vils métiers*, which is to say the tradesmen.'

Winifrede's eyes, like the wheels of a toy motorcar, have been staring eagerly from her healthy fair face; her father is the rich and capable proprietor and president of a porcelain factory, and has a knighthood.

Walburga's pretty hands are folded on the table before her and she looks down at them as Alexandra's voice comes sounding its articulate sweet numbers. Walburga's long face is dark grey against the white frame of her coif; she brought that great property to the convent from her devout Brazilian mother; her father, now dead, was of a military family.

Mildred's blue eyes move to survey the novices, how they are comporting themselves, but the heart-shape of her face is a motionless outline as if painted on to her coif.

Alexandra stands like the masthead of an ancient ship. Felicity's violent fingers attack the piece of stuff with her accurate and ever-piercing needle; she had sometimes amused the late Abbess Hildegarde with her timid venom for although her descent was actually as noble as Alexandra's she demonstrated no trace at all of it. 'Some interesting sort of genetic mutation,' Hildegarde had said, 'seeing that with so fine a lineage she is, you know, a common little thing. But Felicity, after all, is something for us to practise benevolence upon.' The rain pelts harder, pattering at the window against Alexandra's clear voice as Felicity stabs and stabs again, as it might be to draw blood. Alexandra is saying:

'You must consider, Sisters, that very soon we shall have an election to appoint our new Abbess of Crewe, each one of us who is sufficiently senior and qualified to vote will do so according to her own conscience, nor may she conspire or exchange opinions upon the subject. Sisters, be vigilant, be sober. You will recall your good fortune, daughters as the majority of you are of dentists, doctors, lawyers, stockbrokers, businessmen and all the Toms, Dicks and Harrys of the realm; you will recognize your good fortune that with the advance of the century this Congregation no longer requires you to present as postulants the *épreuves,* that is to say, the proofs of your nobility for four generations of armigerious forebears on both sides, or else of ten generations of arms-bearers in the male line only. Today the bourgeois mix indifferently with the noble. No longer do we have in our Abbey the separate entrances, the separate dormitories, the separate refectories and staircases for the *sœurs nobles* and the *sœurs bourgeoises*; no longer is the chapel divided by the screens which

73

separated the ladies from the bourgeoisie, the bourgeoisie from the baser orders. We are left now only with our higher instincts to guide us in the matter of how our Order and our Abbey proceeds. Are we to decline into a community of the total bourgeois or are we to retain the characteristics of a society of ladies? Let me recall at this point that in 1873 the Sisters of the Sacred Heart made a pilgrimage to Paray le Monial to the shrine of my ancestral aunt, headed by the Duke of Norfolk in his socks. Sisters, be vigilant. In the message conveyed to me by our celebrated Sister Gertrude, and under obedience to our Prioress Walburga, I am exhorted to appeal to your higher instincts, so that I put before you the following distinctions upon which to ponder well:

'In this Abbey a Lady places her love-letters in the casket provided for them in the main hall, to provide light entertainment for the community during the hour of recreation; but a Bourgeoise keeps her love-letters in a sewing-box.

A Lady has style; but a Bourgeoise does things under the poplars and in the orchard.

A Lady is cheerful and accommodating when dealing with the perpetrators of a third-rate burglary; but a Bourgeoise calls the police.

A Lady recognizes in the scientific methods of surveillance, such as electronics, a valuable and discreet auxiliary to her natural capacity for inquisitiveness; but a Bourgeoise regards such innovations in the light of demonology and considers it more refined to sit and sew.

74

A Lady may or may not commit the Cardinal Sins; but a Bourgeoise dabbles in low crimes and safe demeanours.

A lady bears with fortitude that *Agenbite of Inwit,* celebrated in the treatise of that name in Anglo-Saxon by my ancestor Michel of Northgate in the year 1340; but a Bourgeoise suffers from the miserable common guilty conscience.

A Lady may secretly believe in nothing; but a Bourgeoise invariably proclaims her belief, and believes in the wrong things.

A Lady does not recognize the existence of a scandal which touches upon her own House; but a Bourgeoise broadcasts it *urbi et orbi,* which is to say, all over the place.

A Lady is free; but a Bourgeoise is never free from the desire for freedom.'

Alexandra pauses to smile like an angel of some unearthly intelligent substance upon the community. Felicity has put down her sewing and is looking out of the window as if angry that the rain has stopped. The other Sisters on the dais are looking at Alexandra who now says, 'Sisters, be sober, be vigilant. I don't speak of morals, but of ethics. Our topics are not those of sanctity and holiness, which rest with God; it is a question of whether you are ladies or not, and that is something *we* decide. It was well said in my youth that the question "Is she a lady?" needs no answer, since, with a lady, the question need not arise. Indeed, it is a sad thought that necessity should force us to speak the word in the Abbey of Crewe.'

75

Felicity leaves the table and walks firmly to the door where, as the nuns file out, she stands in apprehensive fury looking out specially for her supporters. Anxious to be ladies, even the sewing nuns keep their embarrassed eyes fixed on the ground as they tread forward to their supper of rice and meat-balls, these being made up out of a tinned food for dogs which contains some very wholesome ingredients, quite good enough for them.

When they are gone, and Felicity with them, Mildred says, 'You struck the right note, Alexandra. Novices and nuns alike, they're snobs to the core.'

'Alexandra, you did well,' says Walburga. 'I think Felicity's hold on the defecting nuns will be finished after that.'

'More defective than defecting,' says Alexandra. 'Winifrede, my dear, since you are a lady of higher instincts you may go and put some white wine on ice.' Winifrede, puzzled but very pleased, departs.

Whereupon they join hands, the three black-draped nuns, Walburga, Alexandra and Mildred. They dance in a ring, light-footed; they skip round one way then turn the other way.

Walburga then says, 'Listen!' She turns her ear to the window. 'Someone's whistled,' she says. A second faint whistle comes across the lawn from the distant trees. The three go to the window to watch in the last light of evening small Felicity running along the pathways, keeping well in to the rhododendrons until she disappears into the trees.

'The ground is sopping wet,' says Alexandra.

'They'll arrange something standing up,' Mildred says.

'Or upside down,' says Walburga.

'Not Felicity,' says Alexandra. 'In the words of Alexander Pope:

> *Virtue she finds too painful an endeavour,*
> *Content to dwell in decencies for ever.'*

Chapter 4

THE deaf and elderly Abbot of Ynce, who is driven over to the Abbey once a week to hear nuns' confessions, assisted by the good Jesuit fathers Maximilian and Baudouin, has been brought to the Abbey; in company with the two Jesuits he has witnessed the voting ceremony, he has proclaimed Alexandra Abbess of Crewe before the assembled community. The old Abbot has presented the new Abbess with her crozier, has celebrated a solemn Mass, and, helped back into the car, has departed deeply asleep in the recesses of the back seat. Throughout the solemn election Felicity was in bed with influenza. She received from her friend Bathildis the news of Alexandra's landslide victory; her reaction was immediately to stick the thermometer in her mouth; this performance was watched with interest on the closed-circuit television by Alexandra, Mildred and Walburga.

But that is all over now, it is over and past. The leaves are falling and the swallows depart. Felicity has long since risen from her sick bed, has packed her suitcases, has tenderly swathed her sewing-box in sacking, and with these effects has left the convent. She has settled with her Jesuit, Thomas, in London, in a small flat in Earl's Court, and already she has made some extraordinary disclosures.

'If only,' says Walburga, 'the police had brought a

charge against those stupid little seminarians who broke into the convent, then she couldn't make public statements while it was under investigation.'

'The law doesn't enter into it,' says the Abbess, now dressed in her splendid white. 'The bothersome people are the press and the bishops. Plainly, the police don't want to interfere in a matter concerning a Catholic establishment; it would be an embarrassment.'

Mildred says, 'It was like this. The two young Jesuits, who have now been expelled from the Order, hearing that there was a nun who – '

'That was Felicity,' says the Abbess.

'It was Felicity,' Walburga says.

'Yes. A nun who was practising sexual rites, or let us even say obsequies, in the convent grounds and preaching her joyless practices within the convent ... Well, they hear of this nun, and they break into the convent on the chance that Felicity, and maybe one of her friends – '

'Let's say Bathildis,' Walburga says, considering well, with her mind all ears.

'Yes, of course, Felicity and Bathildis, that they might have a romp with those boys.'

'In fact,' says the Abbess, 'they do have a romp.'

'And the students take away the thimble – '

'As a keepsake?' says the Abbess.

'Could it be a sexual symbol?' ventures Mildred.

'I don't see that scenario,' says the Abbess. 'Why would Felicity then make a fuss about the missing thimble the next morning?'

'Well,' says Walburga, 'she would want to draw

attention to her sordid little adventure. They like to boast about these things.'

'And why, if I may think aloud,' says the Lady Abbess, 'would she call the police the next night when they come again?'

'They could be blackmailing her,' Walburga says.

'I don't think that will catch on,' says the Abbess. 'I really don't. Those boys – what are their dreadful names?'

'Gregory and Ambrose,' says Mildred.

'I might have known it,' says the Abbess for no apparent reason. They sit in the Abbess's parlour and she touches the Infant of Prague, so besmeared with rich glamour as are its robes.

'According to this week's story in *The Sunday People* they have now named Maximilian, but not yet Baudouin, as having given them the order to move,' Walburga says.

' "According to *The Sunday People*" is of no account. What is to be the story according to us?' says the Abbess.

'Try this one for size,' says Mildred. 'The boys, Gregory and Ambrose – '

'Those names,' says the Abbess, 'they've put me off this scenario already.'

'All right, the two Jesuit novices – they break into the convent the first night to find a couple of nuns, any nuns – '

'Not in my Abbey,' says the Abbess. 'My nuns are above suspicion. All but Felicity and Bathildis who have been expelled. Felicity, indeed, is excommunicated. I won't have it said that my nuns are so notoriously available that a couple of Jesuit youths could conceivably enter these gates with profane intent.'

'They got in by the orchard gate,' says Mildred thoughtlessly, 'that Walburga left open for Father Baudouin.'

'That is a joke,' says the Abbess, pointing to the Infant of Prague wherein resides the parlour's main transmitter.

'Don't worry,' says Walburga, smiling towards the Infant of Prague with her wide smile in her long, tight-skinned face. 'Nobody knows we are bugged except ourselves and Winifrede never quite takes in the whole picture. Don't worry.'

'I worry about Felicity,' says Mildred. 'She might guess.'

Walburga says, 'All she knows is that our electronics laboratory and the labourers therein serve the purpose of setting up contacts with the new missions founded throughout the world by Gertrude. Beyond the green lines to Gertrude, she knows nothing. Don't worry.'

'It is useless to tell me not to worry,' the Abbess says, 'since I never do. Anxiety is for the bourgeoisie and for great artists in those hours when they are neither asleep nor practising their art. An aristocratic soul feels no anxiety nor, I think, do the famine-stricken of the world as they endure the impotent extremities of starvation. I don't know why it is, but I ponder on starvation and the starving. Sisters, let me tell you a secret. I would rather sink fleshless to my death into the dry soil of some African or Indian plain, dead of hunger with the rest of the dying skeletons than go, as I hear Felicity is now doing, to a psychiatrist for an anxiety-cure.'

'She's seeing a psychiatrist?' says Walburga.

'Poor soul, she lost her little silver thimble,' says the Abbess. 'However, she herself announced on the television that she is undergoing psychiatric treatment for a state of anxiety arising from her excommunication for living with Thomas in sin.'

'What can a psychiatrist do?' says Mildred. 'She cannot be more excommunicated than excommunicated, or less.'

'She has to become resigned to the idea,' the Abbess says. 'According to Felicity, that is her justification for employing a psychiatrist. There was more clap-trap, but I switched it off.'

The bell rings for Vespers. Smiling, the Abbess rises and leads the way.

'It's difficult,' says Mildred as she passes through the door after Walburga, 'not to feel anxious with these stories about us circulating in the world.'

The Abbess stops a moment. 'Courage!' she says. 'To the practitioner of courage there is no anxiety that will not melt away under the effect of grace, however that may be obtained. You recite the Psalms of the Hours, and so do I, frequently giving over, also, to English poetry, my passion. Sisters, be still; to each her own source of grace.'

Felicity's stall is empty and so is Winifrede's. It is the Vespers of the last autumn Sunday of peace within the Abbey walls. By Wednesday of next week, the police will be protecting the place, patrolling by day and prowling by night with their dogs, seeing that the press, the photographers and the television crews have started to go about like a raging lion seeking whom they may devour.

'Sisters, be sober, be vigilant.'

'Amen.'

Outside in the grounds there is nothing but whispering trees on this last Sunday of October and of peace.

> *Fortunate is the man who is kind and leads:*
>   *who conducts his affairs with justice.*
> *He shall never be moved:*
>   *the just shall be in everlasting remembrance.*
> *He shall not fear sad news:*
>   *his heart is firm, trusting in the Lord.*

The pure cold air of the chapel ebbs, it flows and ebbs, with the Gregorian music, the true voices of the community, trained in daily practice by the Choir Mistress for these moments in their profession. All the community is present except Felicity and Winifrede. The Abbess in her freshly changed robe stands before her high seat while the antiphon rises and falls.

> *Blessed are the peacemakers, blessed are the clean of heart:*
> *for they shall see God.*

Still as an obelisk before them stands Alexandra, to survey what she has made, and the Abbess Hildegarde before her, to find it good and bravely to prophesy. Her lips move as in a film dubbed into a strange language:

*When will you ever, Peace, wild wooddove, shy wings
   shut,*
Your round me roaming end, and under be my boughs?
*When, when, Peace, will you, Peace? — I'll not play
   hypocrite*

To my own heart: I yield you do come sometimes; but
*That piecemeal peace is poor peace. What pure peace
   allows*
Alarms of wars, the daunting wars, the death of it?

In the hall, at the foot of the staircase, Mildred says,
'Where is Winifrede?'

The Abbess does not reply until they have reached
her parlour and are seated.

'Winifrede has been to the ladies' lavatory on the
ground floor at Selfridge's and she has not yet returned.'

Walburga says, 'Where will it all end?'

'How on earth,' says Mildred, 'can those two young
men pick up their money in the ladies' room?'

'I expect they will send some girl in to pick it up.
Anyway, those were Winifrede's instructions,' says
Alexandra.

'The more people who know about it the less I like
it,' Walburga says.

'The more money they demand the less I like it,' says
the Abbess. 'Actually, I heard about these demands for
the first time this morning. It makes me wonder what
on earth Baudouin and Maximilian were thinking of to
send those boys into the Abbey in the first place.'

'We wanted Felicity's love-letters,' Mildred says.

'We needed her love-letters,' says Walburga.

'If I had known that was all you needed I could have arranged the job internally,' says the Abbess. 'We have the photo-copy machines after all.'

'Felicity was very watchful at that time,' Mildred says. 'We had to have you elected Abbess, Alexandra.'

'I would have been elected anyway,' says the Abbess. 'But, Sisters, I am with you.'

'If they hadn't taken her thimble the first time they broke in, Felicity would never have suspected a thing,' Walburga says.

Mildred says, 'They were out of their minds, touching that damned thimble. They only took it to show Maximilian how easy it was to break in.'

'Such a fuss,' says the Abbess, as she has said before and will say again, with her lyrical and indifferent air, 'over a little silver thimble.'

'Oh, well, we know very little about it,' says Mildred. 'I personally know nothing about it.'

'I haven't the slightest idea what it's all about,' says Walburga. 'I only know that if Baudouin and Maximilian can't continue to find money, then they are in it up to the neck.'

'Winifrede, too, is in it up to the neck,' says the Abbess, as she has said before and will say again.

The telephone rings from the central switchboard. Frowning and tight-skinned, Walburga goes to answer it while Mildred watches with her fair, unseasonably summer-blue eyes. Walburga places her hand over the mouthpiece and says, 'The *Daily Express* wants to know if you can make a statement, Lady Abbess, concerning Felicity's psychiatric treatment.'

85

'Tell them,' says the Abbess, 'that we have no knowledge of Felicity's activities since she left the convent. Her stall in the chapel is empty and it awaits her return.'

Walburga repeats this slowly to the nun who operates the switchboard, and whose voice quivers as she replies, 'I will give them that message, Sister Walburga.'

'Would you really take her back?' Mildred says. But the telephone rings again. Peace is over.

Walburga answers impatiently and again transmits the message. 'They are very persistent. The reporter wants to know your views on Felicity's defection.'

'Pass me the telephone,' says the Abbess. Then she speaks to the operator. 'Sister, be vigilant, be sober. Get your pencil and pad ready, so that I may dictate a message. It goes as follows:

'The Abbess of Crewe cannot say more than that she would welcome the return of Sister Felicity to the Abbey. As for Sister Felicity's recent escapade, the Abbess is entirely comprehending, and indeed would apply the fine words of John Milton to Sister Felicity's high-spirited action. These words are: "I cannot praise a fugitive and cloistered virtue, unexercised and unbreathed, that never sallies out and sees her adversary, but slinks out of the race ..." – Repeat that to the reporter, if you please, and if there are any more telephone calls from outside please say we've retired for the night.'

'What will they make of that?' Mildred says. 'It sounds awfully charming.'

'They'll make some sort of a garble,' says the Abbess.

'Garble is what we need, now, Sisters. We are leaving the sphere of history and are about to enter that of mythology. Mythology is nothing more than history garbled; likewise history is mythology garbled and it is nothing more in all the history of man. Who are we to alter the nature of things? So far as we are concerned, my dear Sisters, to look for the truth of the matter will be like looking for the lost limbs, toes and fingernails of a body blown to pieces in an air crash.'

'The English Catholic bishops will be furious at your citing Milton,' says Walburga.

'It's the Roman Cardinals who matter,' says the Abbess, 'and I doubt they have ever heard of him.'

The door opens and Winifrede, tired from her journey, unbending in her carriage, enters and makes a deep curtsey.

'Winifrede, my dear,' says the Abbess.

'I have just changed back into my habit, Lady Abbess,' Winifrede says.

'How did it go?'

'It went well,' says Winifrede. 'I saw the woman immediately.'

'You left the shopping-bag on the wash-basin and went into the lavatory?'

'Yes. It went just like that. I knelt and watched from the space under the door. It was a woman wearing a red coat and blue trousers and she carried a copy of *The Tablet*. She started washing her hands at the basin. Then she picked up the bag and went away. I came out of the lavatory immediately, washed my hands and dried them. Nobody noticed a thing.'

'How many women were in the ladies' room?'

87

'There were five and one attendant. But our trans-action was accomplished very quickly.'

'What was the woman in the red coat like? Describe her.'

'Well,' says Winifrede, 'she looked rather masculine. Heavy-faced. I think she was wearing a black wig.'

'Masculine?'

'Her face. Also, rather bony hands. Big wrists. I didn't see her for long.'

'Do you know what I think?' says the Abbess.

'You think it wasn't a woman at all,' Walburga says.

'One of those student Jesuits dressed as a woman,' Mildred says.

'Winifrede, is that possible?' the Abbess says.

'You know,' says Winifrede, 'it's quite possible. Very possible.'

'If so, then I think Baudouin and Maximilian are dangerously stupid,' says the Abbess. 'It is typical of the Jesuit mentality to complicate a simple process. Why choose a ladies' lavatory?'

'It's an easy place for a shopping-bag to change hands,' Walburga says. 'Baudouin is no fool.'

'You should get Baudouin out of your system, Wal-burga,' says the Abbess.

Winifrede begins to finger her rosary beads very ner-vously. 'What is the matter, Winifrede,' says the Abbess.

'The ladies' toilet at Selfridge's was my idea,' she laments. 'I thought it was a good idea. It's an easy place to make a meeting.'

'I don't deny,' says the Abbess, 'that by some chance

your idea has been successful. The throw of the dice is bound to turn sometimes in your favour. But you are wrong to imagine that any idea of yours is good in itself.'

'Anyway,' says Walburga, 'the young brutes have got the money and that will keep them quiet.'

'For a while,' says the Abbess of Crewe.

'Oh, have I got to do it again?' Winifrede says in her little wailing voice.

'Possibly,' says the Abbess. 'Meantime go and rest before Compline. After Compline we shall all meet here for refreshments and some entertaining scenarios. Think up your best scenarios, Sisters.'

'What are scenarios?' says Winifrede.

'They are an art-form,' says the Abbess of Crewe, 'based on facts. A good scenario is a garble. A bad one is a bungle. They need not be plausible, only hypnotic, like all good art.'

Chapter 5

'GERTRUDE,' says the Abbess into the green telephone, 'have you seen the papers?'

'Yes,' says Gertrude.

'You mean that the news has reached Reykjavik?'

'Czechoslovakia has won the World Title.'

'I mean the news about us, Gertrude, dear.'

'Yes, I saw a bit about you. What was the point of your bugging the convent?'

'How should I know?' says the Abbess. 'I know nothing about anything. I am occupied with the administration of the Abbey, our music, our rites and traditions, and our electronics projects for contacts with our mission fields. Apart from these affairs I only know what I am told appears in the newspapers which I don't read myself. My dear Gertrude, why don't you come home, or at least be nearer to hand, in France, in Belgium, in Holland, somewhere on the Continent, if not in Britain? I'm seriously thinking of dismantling the green line, Gertrude.'

'Not a bad idea,' Gertrude says. 'There's very little you can do about controlling the missions from Crewe, anyway.'

'If you were nearer to hand, Gertrude, say Austria or Italy even – '

'Too near the Vatican,' says Gertrude.

'We need a European mission,' says the Abbess.

'But I don't like Europe,' says Gertrude. 'It's too near to Rome.'

'Ah yes,' says the Abbess. 'Our own dear Rome. But, Gertrude, I'm having trouble from Rome, and I think you might help us. They will be sending a commission sooner or later to look into things here at Crewe, don't you think? So much publicity. How can I cope if you keep away?'

'Eavesdropping,' says Gertrude, 'is immoral.'

'Have you got a cold in the chest, Gertrude?'

'You ought not to have listened in to the nuns' conversations. You shouldn't have opened their letters and you ought not to have read them. You should have invested their dowries in the convent and you ought to have stopped your Jesuit friends from breaking into the Abbey.'

'Gertrude,' says the Abbess, 'I know that Felicity had a pile of love-letters.'

'You should have told her to destroy them. You ought to have warned her. You should have let the nuns who wanted to vote for her do so. You ought to have – '

'Gertrude, my devout logician, it is a question upon which I ponder greatly within the umbrageous garden of my thoughts, where you get your "should nots" and your "ought tos" from. They don't arise from the moral systems of the cannibal tribes of the Andes, nor the factions of the deep Congo, nor from the hills of Asia, do they? It seems to me, Gertrude, my love, that your shoulds and your shouldn'ts have been established rather nearer home, let us say the continent of Europe, if you will forgive the expression.'

'The Pope,' says Gertrude, 'should broaden his ecumenical views and he ought to stand by the Second Vatican Council. He should throw the dogmas out of the window there at the Holy See and he ought to let the other religions in by the door and unite.'

The Abbess, at her end of the green line, relaxes in the control room, glancing at the white cold light which plays on the masses of green ferns she has recently placed about the room, beautifying it and concealing the apparatus.

'Gertrude,' she says. 'I have concluded that there's some gap in your logic. And at the same time I am wondering what to do about Walburga, Mildred and Winifrede.'

'Why, what have they done?'

'My dear, it seems it is they who have bugged the Abbey and arranged a burglary.'

'Then send them away.'

'But Mildred and Walburga are two of the finest nuns I have ever had the privilege to know.'

'This is Reykjavik,' Gertrude says. 'Not Fleet Street. Why don't you go on television? You would have a wonderful presence, Lady Abbess.'

'Do you think so, Gertrude? Do you know, I feel very confident in that respect. But I don't care for publicity. I'm in love with English poetry, and even my devotions take that form, as is perfectly valid in my view. Gertrude, I will give an interview on the television if need be, and I will quote some poetry. Which poet do you think most suitable? Gertrude, are you listening? Shall I express your views about the Holy See on the television?'

Gertrude's voice goes faint as she replies, 'No, they're only for home consumption. Give them to the nuns. I'm afraid there's a snowstorm blowing up. Too much interference on the line . . .'

The Abbess skips happily, all by herself in the control room, when she has put down the green receiver. Then she folds her white habit about her and goes into her parlour which has been decorated to her own style. Mildred and Walburga stand up as she enters, and she looks neither at one nor the other, but stands without moving, and they with her, like Stonehenge. In a while the Abbess takes her chair, with her buckled shoes set lightly on the new green carpet. Mildred and Walburga take their places.

'Gertrude,' says the Abbess, 'is on her way to the hinterland, far into the sparse wastes of Iceland where she hopes to introduce daily devotions and central heating into the igloos. We had better get tenders from the central-heating firms and arrange a contract quickly, for I fear that something about the scheme may go wrong, such as the breakdown of Eskimo family life. What is all that yelping outside?'

'Police dogs,' says Mildred. 'The reporters are still at the gate.'

'Keep the nuns well removed from the gates,' says the Abbess. 'Do you know, if things become really bad I shall myself make a statement on television. Have you received any further intelligence?'

'Felicity has made up a list of Abbey crimes,' says Walburga. 'She complains they are crimes under English law, not ecclesiastical crimes, and she has

93

complained on the television that the legal authorities are doing nothing about them.'

'The courts would of course prefer the affair to be settled by Rome,' says the Abbess. 'Have you got the list?' She holds out her hand and flutters her fingers impatiently while Walburga brings out of her deep pocket a thick folded list which eventually reaches the Abbess's fingers.

Mildred says, 'She compiled it with the aid of Thomas and Roget's *Thesaurus*, according to her landlady's daughter, who keeps Winifrede informed.'

'We shall be ruined with all this pay-money that we have to pay,' the Abbess says, unfolding the list. She begins to read aloud, in her clearest modulations:

' "*Wrongdoing committed by the Abbess of Crewe*".' She then looks up from the paper and says, 'I do love that word "wrongdoing". It sounds so like the gong of doom, not at all evocative of that fanfare of Wagnerian trumpets we are led to expect, but something that accompanies the smell of boiled beef and cabbage in the back premises of a Mechanics' Institute in Sheffield in the mid-nineteenth century ... Wrongdoing is moreover something that commercial travellers used to do in the thirties and forties of this century, although now I believe they do the same thing under another name ... Wrongdoing, wrongdoing ... In any sense which Felicity could attach to it, the word does not apply to me, dear ladies. Felicity is a lascivious puritan.'

'We could sue for libel,' Walburga says.

'No more does libel apply to me,' says the Abbess, and continues reading aloud: ' "Concealing, hiding, secreting, covering, screening, cloaking, veiling, shrouding, shading, muffling, masking, disguising, ensconcing, eclipsing, keeping in ignorance, blinding, hoodwinking, mystifying, posing, puzzling, perplexing, embarrassing, bewildering, reserving, suppressing, bamboozling, etcetera."

'I pine so much to know,' says the Abbess, looking up from the list at the attentive handsome faces of Mildred and Walburga, 'what the "etcetera" stands for. Surely Felicity had something in mind?'

'Would it be something to do with fraud?' says Mildred.

'Fraud is implied in the next paragraph,' says the Abbess, 'for it goes on: "Defrauding, cheating, imposing upon, practising upon, outreaching, jockeying, doing, cozening, diddling, circumventing, putting upon, decoying, tricking, hoaxing, juggling, trespassing, beguiling, inveigling, luring, liming, swindling, tripping up, bilking, plucking, outwitting, making believe the moon is made of green cheese and deceiving."

'A dazzling indictment,' says the Abbess, looking up once more, 'and, do you know, she has thought not only of the wrongdoings I have committed but also those I have not yet done but am about to perform.'

The bell rings for Vespers and the Abbess lays aside the dazzling pages.

'I think,' says Walburga, as she follows the Abbess from the private parlour, 'we should dismantle the bugs right away.'

'And destroy our tapes?' says Mildred, rather tremorously. Mildred is very attached to the tapes, playing them back frequently with a rare force of concentration.

'Certainly not,' says the Abbess as they pause at the top of the staircase. 'We cannot destroy evidence the existence of which is vital to our story and which can be orchestrated to meet the demands of the Roman inquisitors who are trying to liquidate the convent. We need the tapes to trick, lure, lime, outwit, bamboozle, etcetera. There is one particular tape in which I prove my innocence of the bugging itself. I am walking with Winifrede under the poplars discussing the disguising and ensconcing as early as last summer. It is the tape that begins with the question, "What is wrong, Sister Winifrede, with the tradional keyhole method . . .?" I replayed and rearranged it the other day, making believe the moon is green cheese with Winifrede's stupid reply which I rightly forget. It is very suitable evidence to present to Rome, if necessary. Sister Winifrede is in it up to the neck. Send her to my parlour after Vespers.'

They descend the stairs with such poise and habitual style that the nuns below, amongst whom already stir like a wind in the rushes the early suspicion and dread of what is to come, are sobered and made vigilant, are collected and composed as they file across the dark lawn, each in her place to Vespers.

High and low come the canticles and the Abbess rises from her tall chair to join the responses. How lyrically move her lips in the tidal sway of the music! . . .

Taking, obtaining, benefiting, procuring, deriving, securing, collecting, reaping, coming in for, stepping into, inheriting, coming by, scraping together, getting hold of, bringing grist to the mill, feathering one's nest . . .

Sisters, be sober, be vigilant, for the devil goeth about as a raging lion seeking whom he may devour.

Glouting, being pleased, deriving pleasure, etcetera, taking delight in, rejoicing in, relishing, liking, enjoying, indulging in, treating oneself, solacing oneself, revelling, luxuriating, being on velvet, being in clover, slaking the appetite, faisant ses choux gras, *basking in the sunshine, treading on enchanted ground.*

> *Out of the deep have I called unto thee, O*
> *Lord:*
> *Lord hear my voice.*
>
> *O let thine ears consider well:*
> *the voice of my complaint.*
> *If thou, Lord, will be extreme to mark*
> *what is done amiss:*
> *O Lord, who may abide it?*
>
> *Happy those early days! when I*
> *Shined in my angel infancy.*
> *Before I understood this place*
> *Appointed for my second race,*
> *Or taught my soul to fancy aught*
> *But a white, celestial thought.*

'The point is, Winifrede, that you took a very great risk passing the money to a young Jesuit seminarian who was dressed up as a woman in Selfridge's ladies' lavatory. He could have been arrested as a transvestite. This time you'd better think up something better.'

The Abbess is busy with a pair of little scissors un-picking the tiny threads that attach the frail setting of an emerald to the robes of the Infant of Prague.

'It pains me,' says the Abbess, 'to expend, waste, squander, lavish, dissipate, exhaust and throw down the drain the Sisters' dowries in this fashion. I am hard used by the Jesuits. However, here you are. Take it to the pawn shop and make some arrangement with Fathers Baudouin and Maximilian how the money is to be picked up. But no more ladies' lavatories.'

'Yes, Lady Abbess,' says Winifrede; then she says in a low wail, 'If only Sister Mildred could come with me or Sister Walburga ...'

'Oh, they know nothing of this affair,' says the Abbess.

'Oh, they know everything!' says Winifrede, the ab-solute clot.

'As far as I'm concerned I know nothing, either,' says the Abbess. 'That is the scenario. And do you know what I am thinking, Winifrede?'

'What is that, Lady Abbess?'

'I'm thinking,' the Abbess says:

> *I am homesick after mine own kind,*
> *Oh, I know that there are folk about me,*
>   *friendly faces,*
> *But I am homesick after mine own kind.*

'Yes, Lady Abbess,' says Winifrede. She curtsies low and is about to depart when the Abbess, in a swirl of white, lays a hand on her arm to retain her.

'Winifrede,' she says, 'before you go, just in case

anything should happen which might tend to embarrass the Abbey, I would like you to sign the confession.'

'Which confession?' says Winifrede, her stout frame heaving with alarm.

'Oh, the usual form of confession.' The Abbess beckons her to the small desk whereon is laid a typed sheet of the Abbey's fine crested paper. The Abbess holds out a pen. 'Sign,' she says.

'May I read it?' Winifrede whines, taking up the papers in her strong hands.

'It's the usual form of confession. But read on, read on, if you have any misgivings.'

Winifrede reads what is typed:

I confess to Almighty God, to blessed Mary ever Virgin, to blessed Michael the archangel, to blessed John the Baptist, to the holy apostles Peter and Paul, and to all the saints, that I have sinned exceedingly in thought, word and deed, through my fault, through my fault, through my most grievous fault.

'Sign,' says the Abbess. 'Just put your name and your designation.'

'I don't really like to commit myself so far,' Winifrede says.

'Well, you know,' says the Abbess, 'since you repeat these words at Mass every morning of your life, I would be quite horrified to think you had been a hypocrite all these years and hadn't meant them. The laity in their hundreds of millions lodge this solemn deposition before the altar every week.' She puts the pen into

Winifrede's frightened hand. 'Even the Pope,' says the Abbess, 'offers the very same damaging testimony every morning of his life; he admits quite frankly that he has committed sins exceedingly all through his own grievous fault. Whereupon the altar boy says: "May almighty God have mercy on you." And all I am saying, Winifrede, is that what's good enough for the Supreme Pontiff is good enough for you. Do you imagine he doesn't mean precisely what he says every morning of his life?'

Winifrede takes the pen and writes under the confession, 'Winifrede, Dame of the Order of the Abbey of Crewe,' in a high and slanting copperplate hand. She pats her habit to see if the emerald is safe in the deep folds of her pocket, and before leaving the parlour she stops at the door to look back warily. The Abbess stands, holding the confession, white in her robes under the lamp and judicious, like blessed Michael the Archangel.

Chapter 6

'WE have entered the realm of mythology,' says the Abbess of Crewe, 'and of course I won't part with the tapes. I claim the ancient Benefit of Clerks. The confidentiality between the nuns and the Abbess cannot be disrupted. These tapes are as good as under the secret of the confessional, and even Rome cannot demand them.'

The television crew has gone home, full of satisfaction, but news reporters loiter in a large group outside the gates. The police patrol the grounds with the dogs that growl at every dry leaf that stirs on the ground.

It is a month since Sister Winifrede, mindful of the Abbess's warning not to choose a ladies' lavatory for a rendezvous, decided it would show initiative and imagination if she arranged to meet her blackmailer in the gentlemen's lavatory at the British Museum. It was down there in that blind alley that Winifrede was arrested by the Museum guard and the attendants. 'Here's one of them poofs,' said the attendant, and Winifrede, dressed in a dark blue business suit, a white shirt with a faint brown stripe and a blue and red striped tie, emblematic of some university unidentified even by the Sunday press, was taken off to the police station still hugging her plastic bag packed tight with all those thousands.

Winifrede began blurting out her story on the way to

the police station and continued it while the police-women were stripping her of her manly clothes, and went on further with her deposition, dressed in a police-station overall. The evening paper headlines announced, 'Crewe Abbey Scandal: New Revelations', 'Crewe Nun Transvestite Caught in Gent's' and 'Crewe Thimble Case – Nun Questioned'.

Winifrede, having told her story, was released without charge on the assurances of the Abbess that it was an internal and ecclesiastical matter, and was being intensively investigated as such. This touchy situation, which the law-enforcement authorities were of a mind to avoid, did not prevent several bishops from paying as many calls to the Abbess Alexandra, whitely robed in her parlour at Crewe, as she would receive, nor did it keep the stories out of the newspapers of the big wide world.

'My Lords,' she told those three of the bishops whom she admitted, 'be vigilant for your own places before you demolish my Abbey. You know of the mower described by Andrew Marvell:

> *While thus he drew his elbow round,*
> *Depopulating all the ground,*
> *And, with his whistling scythe, does cut*
> *Each stroke between the earth and root,*
> *The edged steel, by careless chance,*
> *Did into his own ankle glance,*
> *And there among the grass fell down*
> *By his own scythe the mower mown.*'

They left, puzzled and bedazzled, having one by one

and in many ways assured her they had no intention whatsoever to discredit her Abbey but merely to find out what on earth was going on.

The Abbess, when she finally appeared on the television, was a complete success while she lasted on the screen. She explained, lifting in her beautiful hand a folded piece of paper, that she already had poor Sister Winifrede's signed confession to the effect that she had been guilty of exceeding wrongdoing, fully owning her culpability. The Abbess further went on to deny rumours of inferior feeding at Crewe. 'I don't deny,' she said, 'that we have our Health Food laboratories in which we examine and experiment with vast quantities of nourishing products.' In the field of applied electronics, the Abbess claimed, the Abbey was well in advance and hoped by the end of the year to produce a new and improved lightning conductor which would minimize the danger of lightning in the British Isles to an even smaller percentage than already existed.

The audiences goggled with awe at this lovely lady. She said that such tapes as existed were confidential recordings of individual conversations between nun and Abbess, and these she would never part with. She smiled sublimely and asked for everyone's prayers for the Abbey of Crewe and for her beloved Sister Gertrude, whose magnificent work abroad had earned universal gratitude.

The cameras have all gone home and the reporters wait outside the gates. Only the rubbish-truck, the Jesuit who comes to say Mass and the post-van are permitted to enter and leave. After these morning affairs are over the gates remain locked. Alexandra has received the bishops, has spoken, and has said she will receive them no more. The bishops, who had left the Abbess with soothed feelings, had experienced, a few hours after leaving the Abbey, a curious sense of being unable to recall precisely what explanation Alexandra had given. Now it is too late.

Who is paying blackmailers, for what purpose, to whom, how much, and with funds from what source? There is no clear answer, neither in the press nor in the hands of the bishops. It is the realm of mythology, and the Abbess explains this to Gertrude in her goodbye call on the green telephone.

'Well,' Gertrude says, 'you may have the public mythology of the press and television, but you won't get the mythological approach from Rome. In Rome, they deal with realities.'

'It's quite absurd that I have been delated to Rome with a view to excommunication,' says the Abbess, 'and of course, Gertrude, dear, I am going there myself to plead my cause. Shall you be there with me? You could then come back to England and take up prison reform or something.'

'I'm afraid my permit in Tibet only lasts a certain time,' Gertrude huskily replies. 'I couldn't get away.'

'In response to popular demand,' says the Abbess, 'I have decided to make selected transcripts of my tapes and publish them. I find some passages are missing and fear that the devil who goes about as a raging lion hath devoured them. There are many film and stage offers, and all these events will help tremendously to further your work in the field and to assist the starved multitudes. Gertrude, you know I am become an object of art, the end of which is to give pleasure.'

'Delete the English poetry from those tapes,' Gertrude says. 'It will look bad for you at Rome. It is the language of Cranmer, of the King James version, the book of Common Prayer. Rome will take anything, but English poetry, no.'

'Well, Gertrude, I do not see how the Cardinals themselves can possibly read the transcripts of the tapes or listen to the tapes if their existence is immoral. Anyway, I have obtained all the nuns' signed confessions, which I shall take with me to Rome. Fifty of them.'

'What have the nuns confessed?'

The Abbess reads in her glowing voice over the green telephone to far-away Gertrude the nuns' *Confiteor*.

'They have all signed that statement?'

'Gertrude, do you have bronchial trouble?'

'I am outraged,' says Gertrude, 'to hear you have all been sinning away there in Crewe, and exceedingly at that, not only in thought and deed but also in word. I have been toiling and spinning while, if that sensational text is to be believed, you have been considering the lilies and sinning exceedingly. You are all at fault, all of you, most grievously at fault.'

'Yes, we have that in the confessions, Gertrude, my trusty love. *O felix culpa!* Maximilian and Baudouin have fled the country to America and are giving seminars respectively in ecclesiastical stage management and demonology. Tell me, Gertrude, should I travel to Rome by air or by land and sea?'

'By sea and land,' says Gertrude. 'Keep them waiting.'

'Yes, the fleecy drift of the sky across the Channel will become me. I hope to leave in about ten days' time. The Infant of Prague is already in the bank – Gertrude, are you there?'

'I didn't catch that,' says Gertrude. 'I dropped a hair-pin and picked it up.'

Mildred and Walburga are absent now, having found it necessary to reorganize the infirmary at the Abbey of Ynce for the ailing and ancient Abbot. Alexandra, already seeing in her mind's eye her own shape on the upper deck of the ship that takes her from Dover to Ostend, and thence by train through the St Gothard the long journey to Rome across the map of Europe, sits at her desk prettily writing to the Cardinal at Rome. O rare Abbess of Crewe!

'Your Very Reverend Eminence,

Your Eminence does me the honour to invite me to respond to the Congregational Committee of Investigation into the case of Sister Felicity's little thimble and thimble-related matters . . .'

She has given the orders for the selection and orchestration of the transcripts of her tape-recordings. She has gathered her nuns together before Compline. 'Remove the verses that I have uttered. They are proper to myself alone and should not be cast before the public. Put "Poetry deleted". Sedulously expurgate all such trivial fond records and entitle the compilation *The Abbess of Crewe.*'

Our revels now are ended. Be still, be watchful. She sails indeed on the fine day of her desire into waters exceptionally smooth, and stands on the upper deck, straight as a white ship's funnel, marvelling how the wide sea billows from shore to shore like that cornfield of sublimity which never should be reaped nor was ever sown, orient and immortal wheat.

FOR THE BEST IN PAPERBACKS, LOOK FOR THE

In every corner of the world, on every subject under the sun, Penguin represents quality and variety – the very best in publishing today.

For complete information about books available from Penguin – including Puffins, Penguin Classics and Arkana – and how to order them, write to us at the appropriate address below. Please note that for copyright reasons the selection of books varies from country to country.

In the United Kingdom: Please write to *Dept E.P., Penguin Books Ltd, Harmondsworth, Middlesex, UB7 0DA.*

If you have any difficulty in obtaining a title, please send your order with the correct money, plus ten per cent for postage and packaging, to *PO Box No 11, West Drayton, Middlesex*

In the United States: Please write to *Dept BA, Penguin, 299 Murray Hill Parkway, East Rutherford, New Jersey 07073*

In Canada: Please write to *Penguin Books Canada Ltd, 2801 John Street, Markham, Ontario L3R 1B4*

In Australia: Please write to the *Marketing Department, Penguin Books Australia Ltd, P.O. Box 257, Ringwood, Victoria 3134*

In New Zealand: Please write to the *Marketing Department, Penguin Books (NZ) Ltd, Private Bag, Takapuna, Auckland 9*

In India: Please write to *Penguin Overseas Ltd, 706 Eros Apartments, 56 Nehru Place, New Delhi, 110019*

In the Netherlands: Please write to *Penguin Books Netherlands B.V., Postbus 195, NL–1380AD Weesp*

In West Germany: Please write to *Penguin Books Ltd, Friedrichstrasse 10–12, D–6000 Frankfurt/Main 1*

In Spain: Please write to *Longman Penguin España, Calle San Nicolas 15, E–28013 Madrid*

In Italy: Please write to *Penguin Italia s.r.l., Via Como 4, I-20096 Pioltello (Milano)*

In France: Please write to *Penguin Books Ltd, 39 Rue de Montmorency, F-75003 Paris*

In Japan: Please write to *Longman Penguin Japan Co Ltd, Yamaguchi Building, 2–12–9 Kanda Jimbocho, Chiyoda-Ku, Tokyo 101*

A CHOICE OF PENGUIN FICTION

The Captain and the Enemy   Graham Greene

The Captain always maintained that he won Jim from his father at a game of backgammon ... 'It is good to find the best living writer ... still in such first-rate form' – Francis King in the *Spectator*

The Book and the Brotherhood   Iris Murdoch

'Why should we go on supporting a book which we detest?' Rose Curtland asks. 'The brotherhood of Western intellectuals versus the book of history,' Jenkin Riderhood suggests. 'A thoroughly gripping, stimulating and challenging fiction' – *The Times*

The Image and Other Stories   Isaac Bashevis Singer

'These touching, humorous, beautifully executed stories are the work of a true artist' – *Daily Telegraph*. 'Singer's robust new collection of tales shows a wise teacher at his best' – *Mail on Sunday*

The Enigma of Arrival   V. S. Naipaul

'For sheer abundance of talent, there can hardly be a writer alive who surpasses V. S. Naipaul. Whatever we want in a novelist is to be found in his books' – Irving Howe in *The New York Times Book Review*

Earthly Powers   Anthony Burgess

Anthony Burgess's masterpiece: an enthralling, epic narrative spanning six decades and spotlighting some of the most vivid events and characters of our time. 'Enormous imagination and vitality ... a huge book in every way' – Bernard Levin in the *Sunday Times*

BY THE SAME AUTHOR

A Far Cry from Kensington

'Her story is about principles, literary and other, though love makes a gentle entry too ... The world of Fifties' publishers who, though occasionally crooked, were still gentlemen – dotty, charming and exploitative of clever women – is beautifully recognisable' – Claire Tomalin in the *Independent*

Robinson

'I consider Mrs Spark to be the most gifted and innovative British novelist of her generation' – David Lodge in *The New York Times*

The Ballad of Peckham Rye

'The wackiness is cumulative, the style dead-pan and blow-by-blow, and above all no overt attempt is ever made to get a laugh' – *The New York Times Books Review*

Memento Mori

'This funny and macabre book has delighted me as much as any novel that I have read since the war' – Graham Greene
'Brilliant and singularly gruesome achievement' – Evelyn Waugh

The Girls of Slender Means

'Far and away our best woman novelist' – Penelope Mortimer

The Prime of Miss Jean Brodie

Muriel Spark's sparkling, witty story of the schoolmistress with advanced ideas is without equal.

and

The Mandelbaum Gate
The Go-Away Bird and Other Stories
The Bachelors
The Public Image
The Driver's Seat